Frank Alexander
**The Cyclist**

This is a work of fiction. All the characters and events portrayed in this book are either products of the author's imagination, or are used fictitiously.

THE CYCLIST

Original title: 'De Fietser'

This translation: copyright © 2009 Frank Alexander

www.frankalexander.co.uk

Cover photography and artwork: FAN-Publications

All rights reserved, including the right to reproduce this book, or portions thereof, in any form.

ISBN 978-94-90584-02-3

# The Cyclist

# 1.

There was plenty of manoeuvering space, but the cyclist and the FedEx van didn't move at all. This was mainly due to the cyclist being in the middle of the road, making it impossible for the van to drive onto The Strand.

'Oh, just move!' the driver yelled. He was leaning out of his window and he was waving his arms wildly to emphasise his words. He was a young man, with a boldness that was totally age-related. 'This lane is more than wide enough for the both of us!'

'I couldn't agree more,' the cyclist answered flatly. 'But you are not supposed to drive here and...'

'Please take your lectures somewhere else,' the driver interrupted. 'If anybody tells me what I can and can't do, it's me.'

'I'm sorry,' the cyclist replied. 'But I don't think so.'

He laid his bicycle exactly in the middle of the road to make sure the driver wouldn't all of a sudden accelerate, and walked up to the van. The driver watched him anxiously, for his sheer appearance breathed authority. The man was at least six foot five, moved like an aristocrat and this made him quite an impressive figure.

'Won't you please get out of your vehicle?' the cyclist asked. 'I would very much like to show you something.'

'Oh, come on,' the driver snapped. 'Can't you just act like a normal person?'

But the cyclist waited, unperturbed, and only cast an innocent look at the driver every other four seconds or so. The driver uttered a growl and climbed down from his cabin.

'Alright, let's get this over with,' he snarled. The cyclist walked to the entrance of Northumberland Street and pointed vaguely towards the buildings on the left hand side. The driver looked at him questioningly.

'What?' he asked.

'I suppose you know what that is?' the cyclist answered, and the van driver took a deep breath.

'A road sign,' he said. 'That-is-a-road-sign. Satisfied?'

The cyclist nodded.

'That is the correct answer,' he said. 'But...what kind of a road sign is it? What does it mean?'

'Oh, cut the crap,' the driver snapped. 'And just tell me what you want.'

'I want to go home,' the cyclist replied. 'I simply want to continue my journey through Craven Street, towards Hungerford Bridge and go home. But somehow I think that this is not what you mean.'

'Indeed,' the driver said. 'That is exactly not what I mean.'

'If I am not completely mistaken,' the cyclist gave the driver a piercing look, 'that sign means that no-one can approach The Strand from this direction, except for bicycles being pushed. You have to follow Craven Street, take a left at Embankment Place, follow Villiers Street, turn right into John Adams Street, and then turn left. You see, this is a one way road.'

'Is it? Well, bad luck. I am in a hurry, even more so now, thanks to you and your insane pastime, and I will get onto The Strand via the shortest route possible, which lies straight ahead -whether you like it or not.'

'But sir! What difference does it make whether I like that or not? What matters is that we have rules. What would you have done had I been an unsuspecting little girl, cycling towards you, safe in the knowledge that no motorized traffic can come from that direction?'

The driver sighed and walked back to his van.

'You aren't exactly a little girl. And I've just had about enough. I am in a hurry and I give you exactly ten seconds to get that bloody bike out of my way.'

'And if not?'

'If not, you can walk your way home through Craven Street and towards Hungerford Bridge,' the driver snapped while he got back into his vehicle. The cyclist had followed him and now prevented the driver from shutting his door.

'Do I understand from what you are saying that you neither mind violating the traffic law, nor deliberately damaging other people's property?'

The driver grinned. 'That's a fair summary, I'd say. And what are you going to do about it? Call the police?'

'No,' the cyclist said. 'Heavens, no.'

The driver nodded with satisfaction. He was going to win this battle. He could feel it.

'No,' the cyclist repeated, while the driver started his engine and tried to close his door. 'The police have lost their grip on criminals like you long ago. No, I'm afraid I shall have to discipline you otherwise.'

The revolver was there without warning, looking strangely shaped because of the silencer. The driver stared at the cyclist in utter astonishment. But the cyclist's face was serious and his eyes showed no sign of playfulness. This man meant business.

'Alright, alright,' the driver muttered. 'If you insist...'

'Don't bother,' the cyclist said lightheartedly. 'You'd do it for me, not because you realize that your actions are indeed criminal. And your attitude doesn't fill me with confidence that you will change your future ways. You just don't want to understand.'

The revolver jolted twice and two beautifully round holes appeared around the driver's heart, from which blood instantly began to ooze. The driver looked uncomprehendingly at the cyclist, only to look even more uncomprehendingly at his own chest.

'My name,' the cyclist said as he impassively watched the driver lose his life, 'is Balls.'

He waited until the driver's eyes opened again, put the revolver back into his pocket and slowly walked back to his bike. When he picked it up, he looked around. There wasn't a soul in sight.

'Strange,' he said to himself. 'I could have sworn this was a very lively neighbourhood.'

He shrugged, got onto his bicycle, glanced at the van for the last time, and calmly pushed his bike into Craven Street, towards Hungerford Bridge.

## 2.

*"Children,"* Jim Jeremy wrote, *"are capital punishment. If you get life you can be relatively sure that you will walk free after twenty years, but children really will haunt you for the rest of your days. They have one strategy: making your life as miserable as possible. And they have one goal and one goal only: to put their hands on their inheritance as fast and fiscally lucratively as possible. As long as they depend on you they know exactly how to be at their most annoying, twenty-four hours a day. And once they can think for themselves -whatever the public considers that to be- they know perfectly well how to pull your parental strings and freeload a little longer. They know you will never let them down, because they are your children, your own flesh and blood. You wouldn't reject them for the world.*

*Which is ridiculous, of course. Children are useful for one reason and one reason only -to keep the species alive. There is no reason to add any sentiment at all to that fact. Children don't deserve sentiment. Children deserve only one thing: to be put away in an institution from the day they are born, not to be released from it until they've turned thirty. It is at that age that they may be expected to have a few decent thoughts of their own -not counting, that is, the grey majority who will start thinking about having children at that age..."*

Robert Murdoch was the Chief Editor with 'The Pothole'. 'The Pothole' was a small, well-read but not very highly regarded tabloid that still held office in Fleet Street. Having been anti-political from the start and determined to be specialized in uncovering everything the country's politicians preferred to cover up, there had never been any doubt what it's name should be.

Robert was a young man, always well-dressed and well-groomed, with a perfect shade of a three-day beard. He had charisma and that had been a very important reason to employ him. In recent months, 'The Pothole' had lost quite a bit of its credibility, and Jim Jeremy's daily column had done its bit to assist in its demise. Jeremy was a cynic, at least on paper, and he had shown his skills more than once with reliable venom. Nobody knew why, but from one day to he next something had changed and Jeremy's work got sloppier by the day. His daily column became the most discussed piece, in the office as well as on the streets:

'Did you read Jeremy? Terrible again, don't you think? Makes you wonder why they still keep him on.'

Nobody in the editorial department had the nerve to sack Jim because he was an old-timer, connected with 'The Pothole' from day one, but in the end the Board of Directors had to tell him that he had to get his act together again, or face dismissal.

The turning point came when Robert Murdoch stepped in. He had recognized Jeremy's potential as a writer and an editor instantly. He had taken the pressure off him by changing his daily column into a weekly one, letting him do easy editing tasks for most of his remaining hours. Murdoch had also taken the task of editing Jeremy's column upon himself, so that he could keep an eye on the man without giving him the idea that he was being watched: Jeremy was a good guy, who just needed a kick up the backside every now and then. He had been easily pleased with a new laptop and he had accepted his factual degradation without a word of protest. His articles had become better again, and so had his columns. Robert looked at the one on his desk and smiled broadly. This was good old-fashioned Jim Jeremy stuff. Too bad that the man himself didn't know anything about his potential, that he had no idea that his cynicism was golden... Robert called his secretary.

'Doris? Is Jim still in?'

'No', came the reply. 'He left right away. He said he'd some inspiration, but that he couldn't work in this beehive. Do you want me to try his mobile?'

'No.' Robert knew very well that Jim hated to be called on his mobile phone when he was writing. 'If he calls in again, just tell him that I'd like to catch up with him. That's all.'

Robert got out his red pencil and edited Jeremy's column quickly. He didn't have to correct much. A few typos, one or two words to improve fluency, and that was it. Which was a pity, Robert thought, because after editing Jim's column he had to return to the real news, which basically wasn't there. Summer had started early, it had been terrifically hot outside since May and everybody appeared to be trying to avoid being in the news. No news came from Whitehall or Downing Street for days on end, foreign news had been slow for ages -the only time peace talks did come through, it was usually only a matter of hours before the parties got stuck again- and the local news mainly concentrated on scuffles on the streets, because the heat had made the Londoners even more irritable than usual. It was so hard to make a decent daily paper, that at the latest meeting somebody had seriously asked if turning 'The Pothole' into a weekly paper wasn't an option.

'This sucks,' Robert sighed as he thumbed through the pile of paper on his desk. 'How can anybody expect us to make a newspaper out of this load of crap?'

Giraffe born in Chester Zoo. Page one news for 'The Sun', maybe, but not for 'The Pothole'. Its readers couldn't care less about animals.

Fake hand grenade causes panic on Brighton beach. No. Not big enough. Dead driver in Northumberland Street. Drunken Scots cause mayhem at The Strand Hotel... He thumbed back, thinking that Northumberland Street was an unlikely place for a driver to be found dead.

It was a short piece of news. Driver with two bullets in his heart. Dead at the scene. No witnesses. The driver was not known to the police. No leads.

Robert got on his phone.

'Rumbelow? Yes. That article of yours about that dead man in...yes, exactly. It's the best we have. I need more words, many more, and more information, because it's going to be our leading article. What do I care? Make them say something. Make it up. Whatever. With these temperatures people believe everything you tell them.'

Robert ended the call. It wasn't much, but he had a decent, cynical column, and a dead man with two bullet holes in his chest. Suicide was out of the question, and that made it the perfect headline. Murder, without witnesses or suspects. In the heart of London, in the slowest season of the decade. He smiled at his computer screen. This was almost too good to be true.

# 3.

Ben Dixon hated everything that had anything to do with climate control and he growled when he entered his room. As far as he was concerned it felt like the room was close to freezing. The windows were shut, naturally, and the blinds were closed, all due to that stupid company policy to 'keep the head cool, so you can think properly'. That was utter bullshit, of course. The best ideas always arose when you put seven or eight people into a too small, stuffy and excessively heated room: their eagerness to get away would make them think twice as hard as usual. Air conditioning, ventilators -they all had a negative impact on his job. Ben pulled up the blinds and opened the window. The humid heat filled the room and Ben took a deep and satisfied breath. This was a lot better -it couldn't be hot enough for him.

Ben Dixon weighed twenty-stone, was six foot eight tall, and he was a detective with the Metropolitan Police. He turned around and glanced at the room for the hundredth time. This was where he was supposed to do his job, in a room that wasn't much more than a cupboard, stuffed away in the remotest corner of the Agar Street Police Station. Ben had only just come to terms with his new room in Seymour Street when he was told that he would be transferred to this place, the dullest of police stations, for no other reason than that there appeared to be an increase in drugs related activity in the area. One of the suits had decided that it would be a good idea to use a rotational system for the detectives -to 'keep them on their toes'. Ben was told that his assignment to Agar Street would only be temporarily, and to appease him he was also given the case of the dead driver, found in Northumberland Street. That the Agar Street station also suffered from chronically understaffing was something Ben had only discovered upon his arrival -when he was given a hero's welcome by the few staff members actually around.

'Fuck 'em.'

The words came out strong and deliberate, every time he saw his workspace. Understaffed or not, they hadn't been able to find him a decent room. The upgraded cleaning cupboard they had finally put him in, together with a mobile air-conditioner as if they had done him the greatest of favours, was the worst room he'd ever had. The ceiling was stained with brown spots caused by lights that had been removed and replaced by halogen lamps that looked as though they had been bought at The Pound shop only days ago. The silhouettes of paintings or pictures were still visible on the wall and the carpet was permanently damaged with cigarette burns and assorted, suspicious looking stains.

Ben snorted and looked at his old and battered desk, which was borrowed from the bailiff's office in the adjacent building. It had been hoisted from one building into the other. Ben had witnessed the whole operation, which must have cost a small fortune. The accompanying chair had never arrived, so Ben had taken an old one from the stuffy basement, which he had tried to protect with a tight plastic cover so air couldn't get into the cushion. It was to no avail. Underneath the plastic, mould had begun to develop and Ben thought that it was only a matter of time before the slugs would follow.

The thought hadn't actually left him when the door opened.

'Good God Almighty. Which nutcase opened the windows in here for God's sake? It's like being in the Menali Desert, for crying out loud!'

Ben looked at the man who had entered in disgust. He was fat, his eyes lay deep in his head and his brows looked remarkably similar to feelers. He didn't really walk, but seemed to drag himself along. Ben swallowed. So much for associative thinking.

'Welcome to Agar Street,' the man puffed and tried to make himself look even bigger. 'I'm Superintendent Steerer. I'm sorry I couldn't meet you when you arrived.'

Ben couldn't do anything other than shake the proffered, sweaty hand and when the superintendent scuffed around the desk Ben couldn't help looking at his own hand to see if he could detect a slime-trail.

'Have you ever been to the Menali-desert?' he asked, not having heard of it himself. The superintendent shook his head.

'No,' he answered. 'Low tide in Blackpool on a hot August day is more than enough desert for me. Do you like your new room?'

'How shall I put it?' Ben replied and he made an indistinct gesture. 'It doesn't really feel completely comfortable yet, but I'll work on that. A few pictures on the wall...'

Steerer's jaw dropped.

'I thought your appointment was only temporarily?'

'It is,' confirmed Ben and the smile returned to the superintendent's face. 'But I like to feel at home -even at work.'

'So do I,' Steerer said. 'But it's merely a state of mind, you know? I feel at home wherever I am. That's why nobody will ever be able to accuse me of straying.'

He laughed too loud at his own joke and Ben smiled dutifully. He could sense pretty well what a 'collaboration' with this man would be like.

Superintendent Steerer sat down on the desk chair. Ben could almost see the mould attack the man, panicking to get away from that fat ass, worming it's way through the uniform to nest in his groin instead...he shook his head and ditched the, none too appealing, image. Instead, he waited resignedly for the superintendent's welcome speech.

'I understand,' Steerer said heavily and with overacted pompousness, 'that you were given the shooting that took place on The Strand?'

'In Northumberland Street,' Ben corrected him and regretted it instantly. Steerer cast him a long and reproachful look.

'Never question your superiors, boy, take my word for it. Sometimes you just can't make it on your own, and you'd better have some friends in high places when that happens, wouldn't you agree?'

Ben nodded to confirm that the point was well taken. The superintendent contentedly moved his head up and down, causing his triple chins to make a highly unattractive, blubbering sound.

'The Strand shooting,' he continued. 'What do you know about it?'

'Not much,' Ben confessed, and even that wasn't quite the truth, because he knew absolutely nothing about the case yet. The main reason for that was that, as a principle, he refused to read the only paper that had reported about the killing in the first place.

'Hm,' Steerer muttered, trying to challenge Ben. But he kept silent.

'I advise you to spend a few hours in the archives,' Steerer said finally, when he realized that Dixon wasn't going to say anything else. 'I have requested the librarian to make a nice file with all the latest criminal settlements. The Strand is right on top, and I'm sure you will find plenty of similarities when you check the other cases. These things don't just happen. There's always a pattern.'

Like a snail trail, Ben thought, but he said: 'I will most certainly do that, Sir. As a matter of fact, I will make it my first task of the day.'

The superintendent got up and dragged himself to the door.

'My door's always open, son,' he said. 'And I do mean: always.'

Ben had no trouble believing that. He could sense that Steerer wanted him to become completely dependent on him -even if that, too, was only temporarily.

Ben allowed a considerable amount of time to pass before he set out to find the archives room. When he had finally discovered it, he almost ran into Superintendent Steerer, who gave him a short smile of approval before muttering that he was just leaving.

Ben walked into the archives room with a straight face, but he was boiling inside. Ben Dixon hated these kind of coincidences.

# 4.

Why am I so restless? What is that nagging feeling in my stomach? Something is bothering me, but what is it? It can't be that driver. It was a perfect kill. Agreed, I had one moment of weakness, so I fired twice. But he didn't suffer. I've practiced long enough. Oh, my poor window-dummy. All those holes, all those bullets in your body. But I'll make it up to you. I bought sandpaper, kneadable putty, filler and varnish. You will be as beautiful as you were when I found you, I promise you that. You deserve it. Without you I'd never been as good as I am today.

It had to happen. I was prepared for it. Different situations will follow, and they will become more frequent. I know so, I hope so, for there is a lot to do. But why can't I find peace of mind? I have to loose this annoying restlessness! It could betray me, it could cause me to make mistakes. And there is no just cause for it! My methods are perfect! I haven't made any mistakes yet...too bad nobody can testify for that. But wait, that's it! I need witnesses! The public needs to know why I do this! They have to learn about my magnanimous devotion! If nobody knows about the battle I fight, how can I expect to win it? But what to do? Call the police? They will laugh at me, make jokes at my expense, like they always do. But then what? A newspaper? Of course. I'll write a letter to the press. No. I'll type a letter to the press. Now I know why I could never throw away that old typewriter. That machine is perfect for the job. What shall I tell them...easy now, boy. Don't get reckless. First you put on your gloves, then you take out the paper. You don't want to give them your fingerprints, now do you? Right. Now, take it easy. Type slowly. No mistakes -only amateurs make mistakes in letters. And you don't want to be mistaken for an amateur, now do you? What time is it? Half past nine. That's perfect. It will be almost dark within an hour. That will allow me to deliver that letter tonight, without anybody seeing me. Which paper shall I take it to? It will have to be 'The Pothole'. They will most certainly publish it. They're just the type of presumptuous idiots who'd do that. Focus now, boy. Choose your words carefully. This is good. This is very good. This is going to be a very nice letter, if I say so myself.

***

Tudor Street was totally deserted and the cyclist hardly saw the Vauxhall Astra Cabrio coming, despite the fact that it was modified and converted into a Christmas tree lookalike. Only at the very last moment did the driver notice the lone figure moving towards him, and he finally, had to fully slam on his brakes. The cyclist did exactly the same, praying that his cables could handle the sudden force, and car and cyclist came to a grinding halt within inches of each other.

The cyclist looked at the two people in the Astra. The one behind the wheel was a lad who couldn't be a day over twenty, with crew cut hair, one nose piercing, and at least seven more piercings in his right ear. His bare right arm showed an enormous tattoo of a fire-blazing dragon. The boy was frantically chewing on a piece of gum.

The girl in the passenger seat was most certainly not older than eighteen. Her hair was an unnatural shade of blonde, her eyes were amazingly blue and her, probably quite pretty, face was hiding behind a thick layer of make-up. She looked at the cyclist in honest astonishment.

'I told him not to drive so fast,' she said without invitation, which provoked an angry response from the boy. He lifted his right hand and slapped her in the face.

'Shut the fuck up!' he bellowed. 'You keep your fucking mouth shut! I do the talking! And you,' he now addressed the cyclist, 'when are you going to fucking move? You want me to fucking drive straight through you, don't you?'

He shifted the Astra back into gear and pressed the accelerator down. The engine roared, the car trembled with power, and the cyclist slid his right hand into the inside pocket of his coat. When the hand returned, the gun was instantly in the boy's face; his eyes almost popped out of their sockets, and he froze. The cyclist moved swiftly to the right, clearing the road for the Astra.

'My name,' he said, 'is Franklin Theodore Balls. And you will never again be a dangerous driver.'

He pulled the trigger and the bullet hit the boy right between the eyes. The girl screamed and buried her face in her hands in an attempt to avoid seeing her own death coming. But the cyclist had put his gun away as fast as he had drawn it. All he did was quietly watch, as the boy's left foot slid from the clutch pedal, causing the Astra to jerk forward and accelerate along Tudor Street, until it hit a curb and catapulted itself straight into the window of Jones' Dairy Café-Restaurant. The girl was still screaming when the cyclist mounted his bicycle and happily continued his journey. He now knew that there was at least one witness, and he was quite sure that he had seen somebody else running away into Whitefriars Street as well.

He reached Fleet Street without any more disruptions, put his letter into the box simply reading 'Pothole', and made his way home. He could hear the distant siren of a police car, but the sound was too far away to worry him. The cyclist was happy. Things were going really, really well.

# 5.

*"We live in a terrible city,"* Jim Jeremy wrote. *"Have you ever tried Oxford Street on a Saturday around three in the afternoon? The mob flows around you like a river, roughly running into two directions. That these two flows never change, in course nor volume, proves that these herds of people just turn around at either end, only to plod their way back to where they came from in the first place. Like everywhere else, they have swallowed the lie that 'shopping is fun' whole, and they have mindlessly accepted the vicious circle of not knowing what to do with their time, spending it shopping, and ending up not knowing what to do next when they spend their time shopping. Marketing gurus will emphasize the atmospheric character of it all which, by the way, could be defined with three words: useless, desperate and despondent. Everyone making his way towards Oxford Street should, as soon as he takes his place within the ranks of the masses, be decorated and crowned 'ultimate dumbo'.*

*And that flow of egocentric fossils, who don't want to move an inch, marvelously mirror the way these dumbos live their real lives -all they care about is how not to loose their place in the crowd. Unhindered by any kind of brainpower the masses worship the queue they're in, for it is so ultimately British, and they block the street and the entrance to shops for those few individuals who still do have a job, and are therefore forced to get their shopping done on a Saturday at three in the afternoon..."*

Robert Murdoch smiled when he looked up from the piece of paper.

'Brilliant,' he said to the man who was seated on the other side of his desk. 'Another piece of sheer quality.'

Jim just looked at Robert and the editor could almost hear him think. Jim didn't like to be in this office, and Robert knew that. Jim thought the furniture too modern, too shiny. Too much glass and steel for his taste.

Robert examined Jim for another brief moment. They were of the same tall and slender build, but that was as far as the similarities between them went. Robert wore designer suits and silk shirts and was profoundly proud of his perfectly trimmed beard. Jim was his complete opposite. He usually wore faded jeans and even more faded, oversized lumberjack shirts that hung shapelessly around his shoulders. His hair looked as though it had never seen a barber before. The only thing that was always well looked after, was his face, which was always clean-shaven. Robert suspected Jim to shave at least three times a day and he thought of it as a fascinating contradiction -a man who couldn't care less for appearance, who yet took great pride in shaving.

When asked about his lack of interest in fashion by his colleagues, Jim used to answer with remarks like 'I have better things to do. Writing for instance', which would silence them immediately.

'Yes, thank you,' Jim said, responding to Robert's compliment. 'You never know which way it's going to go until it's finished.'

Robert nodded.

'Still you have reached a new level lately.' Jim squeezed his eyes slightly and Robert couldn't help noticing it. Jim had a suspicious mind, and no matter what Robert did, he didn't think that would ever change.

'Basically it's all thanks to you,' Jim finally said. 'Since it's now a weekly I have much more time to look around and listen. I simply have a better choice of subjects.'

Robert pushed a piece of paper towards him.

'How would you fancy a bit of journalistic investigation?'

A cloud came over Jim's face.

'Three weeks ago somebody was shot in Northumberland Street...'

'That is very old news.'

'It was news then. A whole page of it, but after that: nothing. A dead end, so to speak. But I am beginning to have my doubts now. Did you hear what happened last night? No? Well, hold on. A cyclist killed a driver in Tudor Street. He leaves the passenger unharmed, but she still ends up in hospital because the car was still in gear and it crashed into a Dairy Café.'

'Not Jones?' Jim said. 'Dammit! I always have my lunch there!'

'Whatever, Robert said. 'The cyclist got away.'

'And nobody tried to stop him?'

Robert shook his head.

'There was another witness, but his story is a bit shaky. The guy is a junkie and they think he was pushing something when the whole thing happened, so they're not taking his statement very seriously. And besides, I wonder if anybody would have done something. The man was carrying a gun, remember?'

'There are no more heroes left.' It didn't sound reproachful, it was merely a statement.

'But that isn't all,' Robert continued. 'This morning I found that letter on my desk. Typed, using an old-fashioned typewriter -a Triumph, judging by the font. One strikethrough. Neat, classic layout. I'd like to here what you think of it.'

Jim picked up the letter and looked at it inquisitively. He then produced his glasses, and began to read.

# 6.

"*My name,*" the letter started, "*is Balls. "Franklin Theodore Balls. When you take the time to read this letter thoroughly, you'll agree that I have very good reasons to address you.*

*My generation grew up with decent social norms and values and clear rules. Everyone who didn't stick to them or, indeed, violated them, would be justly punished. A time of clarity, in which everybody knew exactly what to expect.*

*These days, and being a journalist it shouldn't escape and probably hasn't escaped your attention, our world is defined by an outrageous meltdown of social norms, not to mention an ever increasing lack of respect for the law. What makes this situation even more annoying, and for people like me totally unbearable, is the fact that the authorities go with the flow of our declining society, rather than act against it. Only yesterday I saw somebody ignoring a red light, right under the eyes of a police officer. The violator didn't even get reprimanded! My heart bleeds when I witness scenes like that. But let me give you two examples of what happened to me recently.*

*The first was a small incident, a couple of weeks ago. I was cycling along Orb Street when, all of a sudden, the door of a parked Mercedes opened right in front of me. The driver hadn't checked his mirrors to see if there was any traffic approaching. I couldn't completely avoid that door; my pedal scratched it. I got off my bicycle to talk to the man and tell him what he had done wrong, but before I could say a word, the man punched me in the face and yelled at me that I was to pay for the damage I had done to his vehicle. And if not... I didn't wait for him to finish his threats. I got on my bicycle and raced away, as you will understand.*

*A few days later, I had just started to use a zebra crossing in Brandon Street, when I was almost run over by a pizza delivery boy on a scooter. When I went to the police to inform them, they laughed in my face. When I insisted they took notice, they actually made me take a breath test! A breath test! Me! I have never touched a drop of alcohol in my entire life! I couldn't have been any more humiliated. And, as you will expect, my visit to the police was to no avail.*

*For me that was the last straw. For a while I pretended to be a journalist with your newspaper. I apologize for that, but it was the only way to gain access to information I needed, information about how to obtain means that could help me defend myself and society against the growing number of criminals on the road. I now have those means available, lately I have been practicing and I have now mastered the use of a small, but very effective handgun. It makes no difference to me if whether I use it with or without a silencer.*

*Three weeks ago I was cycling home, minding my own business, when I was almost run over by a van, entering a one way street from the wrong direction. The driver did not show any remorse, not even after prolonged pleading from me, nor did he express any intention to change his ways in the future. I therefore had no other option than to punish this man for what he had done. Our beautiful society is going downhill because of criminals like him, who, unfortunately, can be found in all classes. I am sure that the man won't be missed, which fits perfectly with the fact that he was a criminal who got what he deserved.*

*Your newspaper was the only one to cover my noble act, although you kept quite silent after the first day. I fear that this was due to a lack of witnesses, for which I apologize as well. I will be more considerate in the future.*

*I write to you about my motives because I believe you have decent journalists working for you, and they will know what to do. Please inform your readers that they should stick to the law and follow the rules, especially in traffic. When everyone does so, nobody will have to fear anything from me. But I won't hesitate to act again should that be necessary.*

*I trust this information will clarify my position and I do count on your kind co-operation.*

*Yours truly,*

*Franklin Theodore Balls"*

# 7.

'Now what kind of an idiot are we dealing with here?' Jim seemingly agitated handed the letter back to Robert. 'Have we called in the white coats yet?'

'Your guess is as good as mine. I somehow think that last night's incident is connected to this letter, but I don't know how, or when, or why.' Robert looked at the letter, as if he was hoping it would all of sudden produce a real answer. 'That's why I was thinking of you. You can be cynical, even more cynical than this man, if you have to. I thought that, maybe, you could find something in those words that could be a lead.' Was he wrong, or did he see he small sparkle in Jim's eyes? 'Would you fancy that?'

'No,' was the straightforward answer. 'Did you inform the police?'

'No.'

'That seems very sensible. I don't think they would take this letter very seriously. I don't even believe we should take it seriously. We're dealing with a nutcase.'

'That's what I considered as well,' Robert responded immediately, to rule out any suspicion on Jim's part that he hadn't actually considered it. 'Any looney on the street could write a letter like that.'

'Exactly. It could be one our millions of jobless idiots who got bored and decided to have a bit of fun. It could, god forbid, be a prank by one of our competitors, to see if we would fall for it. All of them are capable of pulling a stunt like that, so they can have another opportunity to accuse us of being crap journalists. It could be just the brilliant kind of below the belt stunt that would discredit us once and for all.'

Robert noticed that Jim was focused, yet impatient. Apparently he didn't like that Robert didn't have such a suspicious mind. In truth, Robert had always thought Jim's paranoia to be slightly overdone. It could come in handy to see conspiracies every now and then, but Robert thought it was better to keep an open mind towards everything, especially since nothing was ever what it seemed to be anymore.

'It could be anything,' he said. 'We shouldn't get our fingers burned if we just mention it in the editorial section.'

'Of course,' Jim said sarcastically. 'What are you going to do? Why not put in a classified ad? "Mister Balls, please call again. We don't really trust the letter you sent us." Do you really think that would work? And I'll tell you something else. Franklin Theodore are two well chosen names. Nobody calls his kids that.'

'I don't agree,' Robert said. 'I know at least five people who were named after famous presidents. And I do believe this could make a good story.'

'Maybe. But I think you should stick with the facts. Put that bloody letter in a file and laugh about it when you see it again in ten years time -if you still know where it is. If you need it before then, it may make sense to do a bit of investigating.'

Robert rubbed his beard and looked at the letter once more.

'He didn't sign it,' he concluded.

'Of course not!' Jim snapped. 'His handwriting could give him away within hours. Suppose you publish the original letter and you get a call from Mrs. Beeton, telling you that the signature looks remarkably similar to that of her seven year old nephew? It would make us the laughing stock of Fleet Street. Though, I must admit that the lack of a signature could mean that the letter is real after all, but I also believe we should wait. We will make complete fools of ourselves if we publish it and it all appears to be some kind of joke. There is no way we can get this right.'

Robert sighed and put the letter into an envelope.

'I suppose you're right. I'll try not to lose my patience. But it would be a shame if we lose a scoop.'

'I don't think we will,' Jim shrugged. 'Don't forget the news is three weeks old. Nobody will remember it anyway. Letter, or no letter.'

## 8.

Ben Dixon hated hospitals. In itself that was a bit strange, for all health institutions are overheated by default, but to Ben that didn't outweigh all the other aspects that came with the package called 'hospital': pale faces, screaming children, neurotic old bints and patronizing nurses. Furthermore, you could almost see the bacilli flying around as soon as you had entered the building. It's not just the patients who are sick, was his motto. Anybody working in a hospital couldn't be much healthier.

He reluctantly walked to the reception desk of St. Bartholomew's, which was manned by two men in security outfits. It couldn't get much worse.

'I am looking for Miss Johnson.'

One of the security guards looked at him blankly.

'So?'

'I'd like to know where she is.'

The security guard didn't even blink an eye. His jaws moved, not because he was trying to speak, but because he was chewing a huge piece of gum.

'Where can I find Miss Johnson?' Ben asked again, now rapidly losing patience.

'Yesterday,' the guard said, 'we had about thirty-seven Miss Johnsons, and about another twenty-one Mrs. Johnsons. Could you please be a little more specific?'

'She is eighteen years old, and was brought into your First Aid department with two broken legs. Car accident. First name Stella.'

The receptionist smiled, but then shook his head reproachfully.

'Don't let them hear you,' he said.

'Don't let who hear what?'

'You calling it First Aid!' The receptionist was completely stunned by this apparent display of sheer ignorance. 'It's been renamed A&E ages ago! A&E? Accident and Emergency?'

Ben blinked.

'Of course. And Miss Johnson?'

'Orthopedic ward. Would you know how to find that?'

Ben nodded and hurried away from reception. He hated this hospital, with its old buildings and never completely fading smell of ether. He looked around as if he was afraid that people could hear his thoughts, but nobody paid any attention to him. Ben liked new hospitals, like The New Victoria, with its state of the art equipment and bright rooms. But that wasn't where the action was. The New Victoria was for the rich; criminals and their victims usually ended up in Barts.

Stella Johnson shared the ward with at least twenty other women and Ben mumbled a curse. With so many others listening in on their conversation, it wasn't unthinkable that he wouldn't get a decent statement from the woman. It would be a miracle if they wouldn't be interrupted every other minute.

He didn't have to check all the beds to see which name belonged to who. Stella Johnson was the only teenager amongst a bunch of very old bags, her blonde hair almost blinding, compared with the grayness of those around her. Ben wondered how real the colour of her hair actually was, but he decided it was of no use to find out.

'Miss Johnson?'

She looked up and for a moment he was speechless because of her brilliant blue eyes. He decided that she must be a natural blonde.

'My name is Dixon. Ben Dixon. Metropolitan Police, Agar Street Station.'

Those last words came hesitantly. Why hadn't they just let him keep his office in Seymour Street?

'I'd like to ask you a few things about what happened the other night.'

The girl nodded almost unnoticeably.

'Please call me Stella. I don't like that 'miss' kind of thing.'

'As you please. Can I sit down?' Three days in hospital and the girl had lost all sense of politeness already. He hoped Barts would never happen to him.

'Do you remember anything at all?'

'It all went so fast,' she said, the panic still in her voice. 'He was there all of a sudden...'

'Where did you come from?'

'We came from Bouverie Street. Ollie wanted to get to New Bridge Street...we were a little late, so he just drove...and then all of a sudden that cyclist was there...'

'All of a sudden?'

'Yes. I mean, I had told Ollie that he shouldn't speed, but he never listens anyway, you understand. If I say something like that he hits me, so I know that I have to shut up.'

'Hm.'

'But I am sure he didn't hit that cyclist. Ollie would do anything to avoid damaging the car.'

'What happened next?'

'Well...Ollie wanted to get going again, so he showed off a bit. You know, making the engine roar. He likes that. If the engine is well tuned and you really hit the accelerator...'

'I know, Stella. I own a car myself.'

'Really? Wow. Well, then...that cyclist...he pretended to step aside but then all of a sudden he drew this gun and...and...shot Ollie in the head...and then suddenly I see that shop coming towards me...and then nothing.'

'Did the guy say something? Anything at all?'

Stella shook her head, but stopped. Her hair hung before her eyes.

'Yes, he said that Ollie wouldn't be dangerous anymore. And he mentioned his name.'

Ben looked at her skeptically. The girl had lost it. Nobody introduced himself after he just killed someone.

'He mentioned his name first, and then that stuff about Ollie and being dangerous...Jesus, what did he say again? "My name," he said, "is bla bla bla..."'

Ben kept quiet and just looked at her. Maybe the girl really was trying.

'Uhm...Oh! Yes. I know!' Stella sounded almost cheerful. My name is Frankie Moore. That is what he said. And then he said the thing about Ollie.'

Ben wrote the name down, but added a big question mark.

'Do you remember what he looked like?' He didn't have much hope.

'He looked like a rather nice gentleman. He had black hair and a very short trimmed beard. I think he wore glasses. He looked a bit like a teacher. And he wore a trench coat. That is a it strange, come to think of it. It was quite hot.'

She went silent and seemed to look straight through him. Ben realized that this was all she would tell him, at least today. He put his hand on her shoulder.

'Thank you, Stella. You've been a great help. I may need you again, though, if that is alright with you?'

'What? Oh, sure.' She pointed towards her legs. 'I won't run away.'

He got up and left the orthopedic ward without saying another word. Ben Dixon hated relativising patients.

## 9.

'Shit!'

Robert Murdoch moved away from his mistress when his phone kept ringing. He looked at her beautifully bronzed skin and, for one short moment, considered letting nature take its course, but then decided against it. The phone could bring a scoop.

'Why don't you just activate your voicemail?' the girl grumbled. She had just turned eighteen, was called Debbie and spent most of her days enjoying being a nymphomaniac. She had seen more beds in her few sexually active years than most Londoners in a lifetime, but nobody really cared. Most men were totally incapable of pleasing her for more than two hours, and for the most part they were more than happy for her to have other lovers at hand, so that everybody would benefit from her, and she would benefit from all. Her parents might have had some objections to her lifestyle, but they didn't know any better than that their daughter was still trying very hard to finally gain her A-levels.

Debbie wasn't stupid, but when it came to anything other than sex, she was just utterly lazy. Being a schoolgirl brought her a wild life of almost unlimited freedom. She had dropped a bombshell at home lately, stating that she would definitely aim for a Bachelor's Degree next. Her mother hadn't had the nerve to object, and she was never sure if the news actually got through to her father, who was, as a rule, too busy working. She had successfully talked her mother into doing all the necessary donkey work involved in finding her a decent University, so she knew that she could extend her frivolous life by at least three more years.

While Robert made his way to his desk he thought about the young woman in his bed. His wife didn't even know how to spell the word 'sex'; they were married only because he had money and she was respectable. As a couple they inevitably made a good impression on everybody, which was more than most people could say for themselves. Besides, his job took so much of his time that he was more than happy to just having a few hours of steaming sex with Debbie every now and then. Thinking of that made him run to the phone, to keep the interruption as short as possible.

'Hello?' There was a silence, but then a polite, slightly rigid voice came to life.

'Mister Murdoch? Is this mister Robert Murdoch?'

'It is,' Robert said joyfully. 'Completely.' He looked at his shrinking penis. 'Well, almost. Who is this speaking?'

'My name,' the voice said, 'is Balls. Franklin Theodore Balls, to be exact. We don't enjoy knowing each other personally, but I think you received my letter some time ago...'

'How did you get hold of this number?' Robert interrupted him. The man laughed scornfully.

'I told you in my letter that I have acted as a journalist for some time. If you don't protect your number from being sent, everybody you call will see it in their display. And I do have friends in certain places.'

Robert swallowed uneasily.

'What can I do for you?' he asked, and he lowered the tone of his voice to make it sound more businesslike.

'You know very well what to do. Unless, of course, you didn't really read my letter.'

'I ha-have read your let-letter,' Robert could hardly control his voice when Debbie's nails suddenly teased his buttocks.

'Hurry up,' she whispered.

'Down!' he whizzed back.

'I beg your pardon?' said Franklin Theodore Balls.

'I am sorry,' Robert said. 'It's the cat, you know.' Debbie started nibbling his free ear.

'I did read your letter, mister -uhm- Balls. And I must admit I had serious doubts about it.'

'Do you mean to tell me you question my mental health?'

Robert rubbed his well trimmed beard and decided not to alienate the man too much -yet. On top of that, he wanted this discussion to be over, for Debbie's hand slid between his legs, looking for his, rapidly returning, erection.

'Not at all,' he replied. 'But the letter arrived three weeks after the murder had taken place, when all the facts were out there. Anybody could have written that letter.'

'Murder? Did you say murder? This just penalty -murder?'

'Mister Balls-s-s-s,' Debbie's mouth had found Robert's knob. 'I don't care what you call it. Fact is that everything that was mentioned in that letter could have been written by somebody who was just bo-o-ored.'

'I see. I suspected something like that. You are a good journalist, mister Murdoch. You don't take things for granted. That is why I'm now contacting you personally. I'll tell you what you should do. Call the police. Agar Street Station. As we speak a witness of my latest act of retribution is being questioned by an officer. It happened at Princess Street, off St. George's Road. I had no choice, but I'm sure you will find that out for yourself. Tell them that I called you. Tell them that you don't believe me. You do that, mister Murdoch. And maybe reconsider publishing the letter. Enjoy your evening, mister Murdoch. And stroke the cat on my behalf. It sounds like she's quite a handful.'

The call was terminated before Robert could say another word. He stared at the mouthpiece for a while, and then lowered his eyes. Debbie's big brown eyes locked on to them, and she was determined not to let go again.

'Ah, what the hell,' Robert said. He threw the handset on his desk, grabbed Debbie's head with two hands and surrendered to her completely for the next two hours.

# 10.

Ben Dixon hated witness interviews in the middle of the night. The night was good for only one thing: sleeping. That view had been the reason his marriage collapsed. He and his wife had had sex on their wedding night, which, of course, had caused her to fall pregnant. Almost nine months later Ben had been the father of a healthy daughter, but by that time his paranoia had got the better of him. He would only touch his wife when she was fully dressed and ready to go to work -and even then he always feared that she would change her mind and drag him into the bedroom. It had been a short marriage; one day she had just left. When he came home from yet another long and tiring working day, all he found was a note with her bank account written on it. "For the allowance" was written underneath it. She didn't take much with her; in fact, the child was the only piece of any importance. Ben still lived in the same house, he duly paid the allowance, he sporadically spoke to his daughter and he never saw his ex-wife. That was fine with him. Close family ties were no good whatsoever.

The man seated opposite Ben -the man who was the reason the detective had his night's rest interrupted- was in his forties, like him, but looked quite a bit older than that. He was thin, his eyes lay deep in his head and the black circles under them were astonishingly big, his skin looked tawny.

This man was also very nervous. His fingers kept picking the arms of the chair he was sitting in. If he stopped that for a moment, he leaned forward and absentmindedly played with his rings; a signet ring that was ugly as sin on the middle finger of his right hand and an even more hideous wedding ring on the ring finger of his left hand.

Ben sat up as straight as possible. Next to the skinny man in the chair, who could barely look over the edge of the desk, the detective seemed like a giant.

Ben switched on the small tape recorder he had brought in for the occasion.

'My name is Dixon,' he said in his deep voice. 'Ben Dixon.'

The little man looked up to him in awe, and answered with a terribly squeaky voice.

'My name is Powell. Harry Powell. With two l's.'

'Harry with two l's?' The man gave a shockingly high pitched laugh, so loudly that a chill ran down Ben's spine -and up again.

'Fine, mister Powell with two l's. Can you tell me what happened?'

'Do you think you will catch him?'

'I believe we will, mister Powell. If you would be so kind as to tell me what happened, that is.'

'And what will his sentence be?'

'His sentence, mister Powell, will depend on the evidence we can produce against him. Your statement will be of great help to us. So please tell me, what did actually happen?'

By now Ben had used up all his friendliness. Much to his surprise, Powell did indeed start to make a statement. Ben moved the tape recorder slightly away. He didn't know if he would have to listen to this statement again, but he didn't want to take any risks with his ears. The sound of Powell's voice was almost too much for him already, and the man hadn't even properly got going.

'It was in Princess Street,' Powell squeaked and Ben grunted. Princess Street? Then why in the world was he here? Why hadn't they dumped this guy over at the station in Southwark Street? Why bring him here? Did they really think that he couldn't do with just a written statement?

'We had been visiting friends. They are good friends, you see. We have known each other for more than twenty years. You have to be good friends then, wouldn't you agree?'

'Of course,' Ben replied, although he couldn't figure out how this man had managed to have any friends at all. 'Do you mind if I smoke?'

'I don't. Please do. Maybe...could you be as kind as to let me have one too? My wife doesn't want me to smoke...'

'Of course,' Ben said safely, and he put his cigarettes on the table. Another poor devil who was being ruled, first by his mother, then by his wife. Maybe he should give the man his cigarettes before he left, so he could spend the rest of the night in an appropriate circus of debauchery.

'Good friends,' he repeated while he lit Powell's cigarette. Powell inhaled deeply, and, as he exhaled, looked like he just had an orgasm.

'Wow, there is something satisfying in just being able to do this, wouldn't you agree? I do smoke behind Emmy's back every now and then, but never like this...'

Ben stared at him, and Powell recomposed himself.

'Yes, very good friends indeed. When we visit them, Emmy lets me have a few drinks. Emmy, she is my wife, you understand? Well, Emmy drives us back. She doesn't mind driving that short stretch. We live on St. George's Road, so it's just a short and safe drive, wouldn't you agree?'

Ben nodded. He could see the picture quite clearly.

'She is not a bad driver,' Powell probably hugely played his wife's driving style down, but he didn't seem to be aware of that. 'But she doesn't drive that much. So it doesn't improve very rapidly, wouldn't you agree?'

Ben sighed carefully. He feared that nothing in Powell's life would improve very rapidly.

'But tonight?'

'Tonight? Oh, of course. I'm sorry. I...Well, she was driving, like she always does. She wants to leave Princess Street and turn right onto St. George's Road and...well...I don't really know, to be honest. I tend to believe that she never saw that cyclist coming. He did have lights on his bicycle, though. Those flashing lights, that still work when you stand still. They do attract attention, wouldn't you agree?'

'Of course.' Ben remained neutrally friendly.

'But whatever it was, I heard a bang and the car jerked when she braked. It was only then that I saw that cyclist.'

'Did your wife hit him?'

'No, I don't believe she did. I think he smashed the bonnet with his hand. That is what I think I would do if...'

'And then?'

'He went to her window and pointed out that she had to lower it. Which she did. I could hear her brace herself to tell him something, but he was actually faster.'

Powell sounded quite surprised. He kept silent for a moment, then took another cigarette.

'He started talking straight away. "Good morning," he said. "I know that it's late and I understand that you would like to go home. But could you please tell me what those traffic lights are for?" That was actually what he said. I think that Emmy may not have seen the red light. I think. But Emmy was tired, and she wanted to go home indeed, so she got a bit agitated. She said that she never had caused an accident. She said that she had driven this route for more than twenty years, and that she could still drive home safely with her eyes closed.'

Powell hesitated for moment. His eyes wandered to the walls and focused on the outlines of the pictures that had once been there. His face expressed amazement, but then he shook his head and looked at Ben again.

'Do you know what he said next? He said: "I believe that is exactly what you did, milady. I think you were driving with your eyes closed. And that is quite dangerous." And the next thing I see is that he produces this revolver and shoots Emmy right between the eyes!'

'What about you?'

'Me? I couldn't move. I felt like I was completely frozen. I didn't dare look at him. But he bent forward, and leaned on the door, and I couldn't really avoid looking at him anymore. That would have been a bit rude, wouldn't you agree?'

'Of course.'

'"Tell me," he said. "Were you happily married?" Not 'are'. No! 'Were', like Emmy wasn't there at all! What could I do? He had that pistol and I...and I...well, I thought...well, that maybe he could see if I was lying. I am not a very good liar, you see. So I said: "No. I am not happily married." And then he smiled and put the gun away. "In that case," he said, "I'd better let you live. Good day, sir." And then he mounted his bicycle and just left the scene!'

# 11.

'That's it?' Ben asked. He sure hoped it was. Powell's account had been entertaining, but Ben's ears were ringing like he had just come out of a Motörhead gig. Powell's voice really was utterly unbearable.

Powell stared at the detective.

'I think so,' he finally said. 'I don't believe I forgot anything.'

'Good,' Ben nodded. 'Now, you did see this man. What did he look like?'

Powell drew a heavy sigh.

'You must understand that I didn't really pay much attention to his appearance. He had that revolver in his hand, you see. He held it loosely, nonchalantly. That is scary, wouldn't you agree?'

'Of course,' Ben agreed. 'But I don't expect you to be able to describe him in full detail. Other people have seen him as well,' he desperately hoped that this would prove true, 'and the more we know about him, the easier it will be for us to picture him.'

'I understand. I need to think. Could I have another cigarette, please?'

'Of course. You take it easy. I need to get something anyway.'

Ben got up and left the room.

'Get that man a cup of tea,' he said to the sergeant that was waiting in the corridor. 'And make sure he doesn't leave the room. I'm going to get me some cigarettes.' The sergeant nodded and headed for the coffee machine in the corner.

Ben left the Police station, crossed the street and had to jump aside because he almost got hit by a speeding scooter, and walked towards Charing Cross station. He felt better. The normal buzz of the city in his ears, and time to think. Mister Powell had a very good memory. Too good, maybe. Ben knew that type of man all too well. He would have loved to kill his wife himself, but had been too chicken for twenty years, fearing the consequences should he fail.

When he returned to his office, Powell looked at him gloomily.

'I don't know much more,' he stated. 'Thanks for the tea, by the way.'

'But what do you remember?' Ben sat down and grabbed a pencil. He had forgotten to switch off the tape recorder. It didn't have a counter, and he didn't feel like trying to find the right passage time and time again.

'He had black hair,' Powell said. 'Shiny, black hair. You know what I mean?'

'Long? Short? Blow-waved?'

'No, no, nothing of the kind. Short and neat, split down the middle, just like my father on his grammar school picture.'

Ben thought that remark gave him a terrifying insight into Powell's upbringing, but he didn't mention it.

'Black hair. His eyes?'

'They must have been brown. If they had been blue I would have clearly remembered them. Blue eyes and black hair is quite a rare combination, wouldn't you agree?'

'Indeed.'

'Yes, brown eyes. Regular face. He wasn't fat or skinny, I mean. He looked quite average.'

'Glasses?'

Powell shook his head.

'No. No hat either. Nothing like that. He may have had a beard. But maybe his face was just unshaven. And he wore a trench coat, so I couldn't see his legs. Does that help you?'

'Of course. Haven't you forgotten anything? Anything at all?'

Powell thought hard, and suddenly his eyes twinkled.

'Of course!' he said. 'He shouted his name when he rode off! How could I forget?'

That caught Ben's attention right away. This might be the most useful bit of information!

'He had to shout, you see,' Powell said. 'He was fast and there was quite a distance between us. "My name," he shouted, "is

Benjamin Galls. There was something else, but I couldn't really make that out. Maybe I was too stunned for that. I mean, people don't usually shout their names when they kill someone, do they?'

Ben exhaled with disappointment.

'Are you sure about that name? No Frank or something? It was definitely Benjamin?'

'That's what it sounded like. Benjamin Galls. Is that not possible?'

'Oh, it is possible. Mister Powell, you've been a great help. May I give you these cigarettes as a token of my appreciation?'

'Oh, well. Thank you. Must I go now?'

'Yes, you can go home. This officer will take you there. Can we be of any more assistance?'

'Oh, well. No, that's quite sufficient. Thank you very much. Goodbye, Mister Dixon.'

'Goodbye, Mister Powell.'

Ben uttered a very indecent collection of words as soon as Powell had left the room. Something was wrong with that man. He should be shocked, emotional, messed up even. But he wasn't. Ben thought that it may be a good idea to have somebody following Mister Powell for a while.

And then that name! Benjamin Galls! Even if you were drunk and hard of hearing it didn't come close to Frankie Moore. Ben shook his head. He would have to pay Miss Johnson another visit tomorrow and find out if she was sure her cyclist called himself Frankie Moore and not Aladdin Sane, or whatever else! Benjamin Galls!

He didn't exactly know why, but he got the feeling that somebody was playing games with him. Ben Dixon hated playing games.

## 12.

'Have you gone mad?' Jim Jeremy could just swallow the F-word. Lucinda didn't like it when he swore. He glanced at the display of his alarm clock. A few minutes pas five in the morning. He had just fallen asleep when that bloody mobile went off. 'Do you really think that I want to be called by you in the middle of the night?'

Beside him the sheets rustled and the bedside lamp was switched on.

'Who is that?' Lucinda asked. Jim waved his hand to silence her, his lips forming the word 'Robert'. Lucinda nodded with understanding. She, too, thought it was desirable not to let her husband know whose bed she shared more than just a few nights a week.

'I must talk to you!' Jim could sense the light panic in Robert's voice. 'This is really urgent!'

'It'd better be,' Jim said. 'Is it a scoop? Only for a scoop will I consider leaving my love nest.'

'It's the continuing story,' Robert replied. 'We had the scoop a while ago.'

'Alright then.' Jim gave up his resistance. 'Where do we meet? At your place?'

'No way. This is work. I meet you at the office in fifteen minutes.'

'Sure. And you think I can make that? Give me half an hour. At least.'

'Fine.' The connection was cut off and Jim drew a deep sigh and looked at the beautiful woman in his bed.

'That husband of yours is developing journalistic tendencies,' he said. Lucinda smiled.

'I'm happy to hear that he is developing anything at all. Are you're going to be away for long? I was quite looking forward to breakfast.'

'I haven't got a clue about his intentions. I'll call you as soon as I can get away -but that may mean you're going to have to wait until lunchtime.'

'Just keep in mind that I will be hungry enough for two by then.' Lucinda switched off the light and went back to sleep, leaving Jeremy speechless for a long moment. But then he smiled, and wondered what in the world had made her choose Robert in the first place. She was so unpretentious, so completely lacking the arrogance that made Robert such a prick.

He felt around the bed to pick up his clothes and made his way into the kitchen, where he got dressed. He counted back the hours that had passed between his last pint and this unholy hour, and came up with three hours and a few minutes. He figured it would be quiet on the streets, and he decided to take the risk. He picked up his car keys and quietly left the house.

## 13.

Robert was caught off guard when Jim entered his office, but he recomposed himself quickly, figuring that what had startled him was the fact that he'd never seen Jeremy before when he'd just been dragged from his bed.

'Is everything alright?' he asked neutrally. Jim lowered himself in a chair.

'Man,' he sighed. 'You'd better appreciate me being here. I really thought my last hour had come!'

'I must admit you look like shit. What happened?'

'I was driving up here, and I was thinking that it is impossible to see the stars due to all the light pollution. So inspiration hit me, and in my head I was writing this column, you know, harshly attacking the councils for denying us that piece of beauty...well, it was one of those pieces that was finished before I'd even put a pen to paper. I need a stiff drink, Robert. Is that possible?'

'No problem.' Robert opened a cupboard and produced a bottle of Scotch.

'So what happened?'

'I was slightly absent-minded when I approached Poultry, so I was speeding a little when I wanted to turn left...and all of a sudden I see this cyclist who is clearly intending to go straight ahead! I had to slam on the brakes and it was a very near miss. He hit the curb, and he didn't completely fall over, but it was a close call. I wanted to get out and apologize when he got up...' Jim gulped his whisky down, '...while he was getting up he was reaching inside his coat and he gave me a look that said that I wasn't going to get away with anything...I just knew this was wrong. I reversed, steered clear of him and got the hell away from there. I checked the mirror once -he was staring at me, his hand still in his pocket...I swear I broke a couple of records getting here. It wasn't until I reached the junction with New Bridge Street that I eased off of the accelerator.'

He shook his head and downed the rest of his whisky.

'But I only felt completely safe when I came inside, can you believe that? I took my time to relax before I got up here; I'm sure you understand. I can only hope he didn't see my licence plate.'

Robert was fascinated by Jim's story.

'What did he look like?'

'I didn't really pay that much attention to him. He was wearing a trench coat. One pretty much like the one you have right there.'

Robert rubbed his well-trimmed beard.

'It makes you wonder if that guy ever sleeps,' he said.

'What do you mean?'

'I received a phone call earlier this night,' Robert replied. 'From a man called Franklin Theodore Balls.' Jim frowned.

'He told me that it hadn't surprised him that we didn't publish his letter. He also told me that this was the reason he made the call. He said there was another victim, although that wasn't his choice of words. And he said that if I called Agar Street Police Station, all would become clear.'

'Did you call them?'

'No. I still don't know what to think of this mess.' Robert didn't feel like explaining that he had spent a few hours with a hot blonde before returning to his work. So he just went on: 'I don't like to talk about things when they are as vague as this. There are nine listed Balls in the London area. All of them decent citizens, none of them initialed FT.

Jim shook his head.

'And that surprises you? This whole name is made up. He picked a combination that sounds good, and that's it. To put it differently: this guy has got balls, and he uses them to make his point. I like that.'

Robert hid his embarrassment, but inside he was cursing. He should have thought of that himself!

'Still,' he said, trying to make the best of the situation. If I add what you just told me to the situation it seems more likely that the whole thing is true after all.'

'It seems so,' Jim admitted. He bit his lip and his eyes wandered off to Robert's trench coat. 'I think you should give the guys in Agar Street a call. You won't have to tell them everything. Leave the name out, for one thing. Just tell them that some nutcase called you to give you this crazy story, that somehow had a ring of truth around it; and that you'd like to check your facts before ditching it. After all, you are a journalist...'

'What about that letter?'

Jim shrugged.

'There's always a chance they want to see it.'

Robert thought about that. If he presented the letter just like that, he would lose his advantage, just when he could reel them in. 'The Pothole' wasn't very popular with the Metropolitan Police, and this seemed to be a golden opportunity to change that. But he would only give them all the pieces of the puzzle if they leveled with him first. That would be fair, and he would find a way to make that work.

He rubbed his well-trimmed beard. He was on the brink of befriending the cops, and he could already see the haunting headlines of tomorrows edition. He picked up the phone.

'What's their number?'

'Just try the Internet,' Jim answered, while taking the bottle of whisky from the desk and pouring himself another drink. 'They like to advertise themselves these days. Unless you want me to find the last hard copy phone book -which was published ten years or so ago and is now considered to be some kind of a collector's item.'

Robert ignored him, and switched on his computer. Jim relaxed in his chair, sipping whisky, and smiling confidently.

# 14.

Ben Dixon hated journalists. They were everywhere, all the time. They emerged in the strangest places and at the worst possible moments. They always thought that their questions were better and more to the point than his, and some of them actually said so out loud! Journalists always thought they were right, they were convinced that obstructing justice was the most important part of their job, and they had no respect whatsoever for anything or anyone. Journalists, in short, were the bane of Ben's existence.

But the one that was seated opposite of him had a point, and what was worse, he had a good point. He somehow had more information about that cyclist than Bed did. It did worry Ben that this moronic publicity whore took more pride in informing the press than in informing the police. If he should continue to do so, Ben may be trailing that idiot for years to come, without ever coming close to catching him. Then, all they could do was wait until some kind of junior editor would arrive in the morning, handing them the synopsis of what would hit the papers within a few hours. Ben could see the headlines: 'Brave journalist dwarfs Metropolitan Police', or even worse 'Journalist arrests criminal while Metropolitan Police watches'. He couldn't let it come to that.

So Ben duly listened to what Robert Murdoch was telling him, meanwhile trying to find a weak spot that would allow him to overtake this arrogant shit head and get one step ahead of him. Which was all he needed.

'The letter,' Robert Murdoch ended his story, 'had not been signed.'

Ben gruntled and ignored the questioning look Murdoch cast him. But since Murdoch didn't have anything else to say, it was now up to the detective to keep the conversation going.

'The gentleman we are chasing,' he said, 'introduced himself at least twice, but with completely different names. He doesn't mention his name when he talks to you…of course it is part of his modus operandi to just pick random names from the telephone book, but I'm sure we could find a pattern…'

He left the rest of his thoughts unspoken. He would be crazy to share his vulnerabilities with a parasite from the press.

'It goes without saying that I want you to keep us informed,' Ben now continued, although he didn't think any journalist could be of any help whatsoever. 'I don't read your newspaper, and I'd like to get my information first hand anyway.'

'One doesn't exclude the other,' Robert said. 'I would be more than happy to offer you a free subscription to 'The Pothole'.'

'As I said,' Ben answered dryly, 'I don't read that paper. And there is something else, mister Murdoch. I'd like you to hand in the original letter. That is a piece of evidence.'

'Of course,' Robert said. 'But I'm afraid it won't be that much of a help. Since we didn't take it very seriously at first, we weren't very cautious. It's safe to say that almost everybody has read the letter, so you'll find my colleagues' fingerprints all over it. I'm sorry.'

Ben discarded his remark with a simple gesture. It was useless to get agitated about it, no matter how mad it drove him that people didn't appreciate evidence when they held it in their hands. But he was dealing with a journalist, and they just couldn't be trusted. Ben also realized that he was a beggar, not a chooser. Obtaining that original letter was basically all he could aim for.

'We filed the letter,' Robert continued. 'I'll have to file a request to get it back. I think I can have it on your desk the day after tomorrow. Can you live with that?'

Ben wondered if he could get away with strangling this chesty imbecile, but decided against it. No journalist was worth it to die by the hands of a man. That would just be too convenient. So he just nodded and smiled as pleasantly as possible.

'That is fine,' he said. 'I'll count on it then. The day after tomorrow. Are you sure you told me everything?'

Robert thought deeply for a while, then shook his head.

'There's nothing more,' he said. 'That is really it.'

Ben nodded and showed him out. Robert turned left on The Strand and headed for the Crown Café. He ordered a double espresso with the very good looking waitress, got out his cell phone and called Jim Jeremy.

## 15.

'Well god-dammit!' Jim Jeremy didn't care about his language this time. 'This is the second time today you interrupt me having sex! This had better be good, Murdoch. Really good.'

'The peeler you sent me to,' Robert was happy to at least share the blame, 'wants the original letter.'

'So? Give it to him. Have you ever noticed that expensive machine in the corner of our department? If you put one piece of paper into it and press a button, it produces an exact lookalike. It's called a copier. Did you really need to call me for that? Thanks a bloody lot.'

'No!' Robert yelled. 'Wait!'

'No, you wait.' Robert heard a bump when the phone apparently hit the floor, and although he couldn't really make out what happened on the other side of the line, the muffled sounds were suggestive enough. It took a good few minutes before everything went completely quiet, and at least another two minutes before the phone was picked up again and Jeremy's voice returned.

'I couldn't control myself any longer. Are you still there?'

'Yes.'

'Too bad. Anyhow, I really don't understand what the fuss is all about. I thought you were the intelligent one? If we are to publish that letter, do you think our readers are going to be able to tell the bloody difference between the original and the copy?'

'That's not the point. I didn't tell him everything.'

'That wasn't very smart.'

'Not very smart? Who suggested I'd leave the name out in the first place?'

Jim drew a heavy sigh.

'When was the last time you were out in the field? Ah, forget it. Now what do you want, exactly?'

'Are you talking to me, or to your sex partner?'

'If I was talking to my sex partner, I'd tell her what I want. I'm talking to you. My chief editor.'

'I want you to do an editorial on that cyclist. And a column. On my desk by four this afternoon, or in my inbox. And do you have any suggestions for a headline?'

'How about "He's got Balls"? Now, if you'll excuse me, I have two articles to write. And when I'm done, I'll come back to this lovely lady and make up for all she's missing out on thanks to you. If I were her, I would hate you for it. But when I'll make up with her later on, I assure you that my phone will be switched off all the time. Cheers.'

Robert got up and walked back to the office, thinking what the best approach would be. He dug up the letter from the paper's archive, took a few blank pages from the recycling bin next to the printer, and went home, where he went straight into his study. In one corner he still had his first typewriter on display, an ancient Triumph. He had always cherished this machine and now he knew why, for when he slipped the paper into it, it went in as smoothly as if the typewriter had only been used yesterday.

He concentrated on the job ahead of him. Letter by letter he copied the cyclist's missive, omitting the pieces he hadn't told Ben Dixon. It became a perfect letter. Even the font matched the original.

He would have to get rid of the typewriter now, even though he didn't like that. But this was for a greater cause, and it was a sacrifice he was prepared to make in order to establish a bond of confidentiality with the Metropolitan Police. And sell a few extra copies of 'The Pothole', of course.

When he had finished he examined both letters closely, and smiled happily. Nobody would ever know the difference. He folded the original letter and put it into his wallet. The newly typed copy went into his inner pocket, ready to be delivered to the desk of Ben Dixon.

Robert cleaned everything up and carried the heavy typewriter into his car. He got in and drove across the city until he reached Chelsea Bridge, which was as quiet as he hoped it would be at this time of day. He parked his car in the bus lane, took the typewriter out and balanced it on the parapet. He took a deep breath and looked at Battersea Power Station on the other bank, its facade mirrored by the river. He thought that it could be a good idea to do a series of articles on landmark buildings in London -and decided to give that a bit more thought later on.

He looked down. No kids, no boats, nothing. He drew a last deep sigh, pushed the typewriter away and followed its fall with his eyes. The machine plunged into the Thames, but it didn't make real waves.

Only when he looked up again did Robert see the lanky youth next to him, who was still looking down with great interest.

'Nope,' the boy said after about twenty seconds. 'A clear miss. If I were you I'd try a more traditional fishing rod next time.' He winked and walked away, leaving Robert dumbfounded on the pavement.

# 16.

*"Cynicism,"* Jim Jeremy wrote, *"is beautiful, although not everybody understands it. Some people just laugh at jokes without ever getting their deeper meaning. Others see that deeper meaning in everything they hear or see. That is freedom, and within that freedom cynicism is a tool that everybody can use freely.*

*It becomes a different matter, though, if the same cynicism becomes a weapon, rather than a tool. And when it is a lunatic that handles the weapon, things become irksome, not to mention threatening.*

*Our beautiful city is haunted by a moron who turns us all into paranoid creatures. As if it is not enough that we are under a constant threat of terrorism, this man has killed three people in cold blood, for no other reason than that they, allegedly, violated a traffic rule.*

*Where will the madness stop? Do we really have to behave like a beaten dog, every time we cross the street? Do we really have to be afraid when we accidentally step outside a zebra crossing's limits? What will happen if we try to avoid a playing toddler and, in doing so, bump into a cyclist? Do we sign our own death warrant?"*

Robert continued reading, thinking that the angle Jim Jeremy had taken was the right one. But serious pieces had never been Jeremy's best features and this wasn't an exception. His column, however, had been one of his best ever. The title 'Bicycle Race' was somewhat of a give away, in the respect that Jeremy had chosen to write the piece from the cyclist's point of view - 'I want to ride it where I like'. In doing so, it appeared to be one long argument in favour of the man and his motives, but between the lines there was subtle sarcasm, so subtle it went almost unnoticed, clearly forcing the reader into realizing that the cyclist lacked quite a bit of common sense.

Either way, the readers would be affected and it would at least make them reconsider their behaviour for a change. Three killings in a relatively short time was too much for comfort, and nobody knew what the man was really capable of. His victims so far had been easy targets, lone people on quiet moments. Maybe that was all it would ever be, but maybe not. People should realize that criminals like the cyclist were unpredictable. What Jim wrote was true: you could indeed be at risk for crossing the street beside a zebra crossing, even if that was only because there were just too many people on it.

It was a good thing that these two articles would be featured in the paper as well. The leading article was brilliant, good old Pothole sensationalist journalism. 'HE'S GOT BALLS' was printed in the largest possible font with the smallest side margins, and the content lived up to that headline; it was sensational, intimidating, indoctrinating.

Robert knew that publishing the other pieces, showing that 'The Pothole' did not just think about its sales figures but also did accept its social responsibility, would do the paper no harm. Those pieces would be on page three, along with the pin-up and the cyclist's letter, which would be published 'complete and uncensored'. Nobody knew that that was not entirely true.

That was to say...hardly anybody knew that that was not entirely true.

# 17.

What happened to my ideal? Why don't people take my noble work more seriously? Why don't things change in traffic? What else can I do to convince them?

Careful, sir, watch out. You're swaying a bit. You are now driving on a designated bicycle lane. And you brake very abruptly. Are you drunk? Ah, I see it now. You are having a conversation on your mobile phone. So you've only got one hand available to switch gears and hold the steering wheel. And you can't really keep an eye on the traffic, for when you look into your mirror, your phone will drop to the floor. Yes, that's quite professional behaviour. And you don't really care that this very behaviour causes dangerous situations for decent road users. Of course, business. No doubt you can make a lot of money doing your business. But that is not my concern. Yes, you are right. Business is business. But I am right as well. The law is the law. Using a mobile phone while driving is an offence. Everybody does it? Really? And would you also commit suicide if everybody all of sudden decided to do that? You think that this is a poor comparison? Well, I don't. Don't be afraid, sir. I know where your heart is located. Unless, of course, you are one of those very few people that has 'situs inversus'. That means your heart is on the wrong side of your chest, sir. No, I thought not. Goodbye, sir. You have just finished your last conversation...

All I want is to safely use the public roads. I don't want to have to anticipate cars emerging from streets they are not suppose to be coming from in the first place. I hate the aggression. I can't walk anywhere without bumping into hurrying idiots, who will then tell me off because I didn't step aside quickly enough. There is not one bicycle lane safe to use, because people use them as parking spaces, or race tracks for scooters and motorcycles. And I have lost count of the times I have been called names because I pointed out to someone that you have to signal before turning left or right.

I have no choice, I am on a mission. Sooner or later people will realize that I am serious. I'll have to think. Should I send another letter to the paper? No, that's too much trouble. Should I change my tactics? Use stronger methods? And what would happen if I do? How do I get the point across that it is still me who's trying to make his point, and not some kind of copycat? It would be a bit tricky to hand out leaflets at Covent Garden; they would arrest me within minutes on the suspicion of acting as an accomplice -at the very least. I don't want to be arrested. Not for acting as an accomplice. Not for committing murder either, by people who don't understand that shooting a criminal is not a crime, but plain justice. And I don't want to be arrested for running a red light either. I want is to ride my bicycle, and I want to be able to safely use the public roads. I want everybody to be able to do that.

## 18.

Ben Dixon hated it when his work piled up. Even though by now he had a big team of detectives working for him, it still looked like finding the cyclist was labour totally lost.

For since the cyclist had shot a prominent businessman because the man was driving and using his mobile phone at the same time, it seemed that the whole of London had developed maniacal tendencies. Londoners had taken the cyclist's acts, as well as the publicity he received, as a license to use violence wherever and whenever they felt like it; branding it 'necessary violence' to link it to the 'mission' the cyclist had mentioned being on.

People weren't safe on public roads anymore. Car drivers literally put their foot down when they saw a bicycle without proper lights, pedestrians threw stones at windshields when car drivers tried to pull up before they had completely crossed the road. Cyclists joined the ranks bravely; one room in Agar Street Police Station was filled with mirrors, kicked off cars by cyclists who demanded more passing space. Even one of the Met's BMW's had become a victim, when it was kicked by a pedestrian who made it very clear that he thought he could still cross the road, even though the car was in full pursuit and had only managed to come to a standstill within an inch of the man.

It it wasn't restricted to a manageable area anymore either. Incidents were reported all over the city, from Brixton to Camden, from Lambeth to Islington. In the polls London now ranked as the unsafest place in Britain by far, and the 2012 Olympic Committee was beginning to get nervous.

Ben heard a distant blow, like an explosion, and waited for a moment to determine if the incident would likely end up as another report to land on his desk. It probably would, for his colleagues had taken on the attitude that everything that happened on public roads had to be connected to the cyclist - making it his problem, all the while keeping their own desks beautifully empty. It was up to Ben to decide who would have to deal with what. The detective was surrounded by files and huge stacks of paper, and the workable space on his desk wasn't much more than half a square yard; just enough for the phone and a notepad. He kept his pen in his pocket, for he lost at least seven in the mess that was called 'evidential back-up'.

The cyclist himself was very active as well, which was probably caused by the hyperactivity of his fellow Londoners. The number of traffic victims who had a small hole in their head or their heart had increased dramatically. Technically, it was still more speculation than knowledge, but postmortems invariably proved that all the bullets came from one and the same gun. Furthermore, the man still reported all his acts to 'The Pothole'. Not by letter, like he did in the early days, but by telephone. Ben wanted to tap Robert Murdoch's phone, but Murdoch had objected vehemently, claiming that he made a lot of confidential phone calls which were of no concern to the Metropolitan Police whatsoever. Since it had been made very clear that their was no evidence that the cyclist was a Muslim, Ben was also told that he could not use the Terrorist Act to get his way, so he had to rely on the court to obtain what he needed. His request to tap Murdoch's phone without the man's co-operation had landed on a pile of paper, marked 'Urgent', which was about as high as the stacks in his own office. Ben wondered how anybody could ever solve a case with this lack of support from the system, and his admiration for colleagues who actually had, grew considerably.

All Ben could do was wait until Murdoch called to tell him where the cyclist had struck again. According to Murdoch, the message was always the same, except of course for the location. 'I have just punished a young man for dangerous driving by shooting him in the head. You will find him…' and then the location would follow. Sometimes a response car was already on its way, but, in almost fifty percent of the cases that didn't happen, because fewer and fewer people had the stomach to actually call the police. Half the city may be running riot, the other half was definitely very frightened.

Ben looked at the smallest pile of paper, which contained all the information on the victims that had ended up with a 7.65 millimeter hole in them. There were thirty-two in total, they had been found all over the city, and that was all they had in common.

'Am I interrupting anything?' Superintendent Steerer pretended to stand on his toes to be able to see him; Ben just shook his head.

'Please, do sit down,' he said, but Steerer declined the invitation.

'No,' said his superior. 'I can't see you when I'm sitting down. And I like to see people when I'm talking to them.'

Ben wanted to reply that, in this case, the feeling wasn't mutual, but he swallowed his words. He didn't think the Superintendent was here to pay him any compliments, and he didn't want to estrange the man any further.

His superior walked towards the mobile air conditioner and switched it on. A loud humming filled the room, and the Superintendent remained close to the cool draught that began to come from the machine.

'It's not going very well, now is it?' Steerer didn't try to hide his revulsion. 'You are, almost literally, up to your neck into it. And I did my best to help you. Did you even look at that brilliant file I had the librarian put together?'

'That file was based on prejudice, non-existing mafia connections and mostly retired drug dealers, sir,' Ben answered. 'It didn't contain that many useful leads.'

Even that was highly exaggerated, he thought. He had found one clue, and not even a very good one, after wading through a thousand pages of information.

'I don't think so, son. I think that you are the one who is following false presumptions.'

His superior rounded the desk and stood beside him. Ben tried to find a silvery trail behind him, but it wasn't to be.

'I saw you and that Murdoch together the other day,' Steerer said. 'What did he want?'

'He had received a letter he thought we would be interested in, sir.' Ben remained polite. 'They published the letter afterwards.'

'I know,' Steerer said. 'In the tabloid that is responsible for all of this.' His arms made a huge circle as if he wanted to embrace the whole city. 'The moment they started reporting on that uncanny cyclist, they really released the elephant.'

Uncanny, Ben thought. Releasing the elephant. The man sure had his way with words.

'I don't think the paper can be blamed for these outbursts, sir. There are always individuals who take their inspiration from what they read in the papers. And all papers report on the cyclist.'

'There are about 3.5 million individuals who take their inspiration from these papers, son. And do you have any idea how the papers are reporting on the case? They are ripping us to shreds, each and every day! The city's getting a terrible reputation on their account. We're losing tourism faster than we can chase it away with our prices, only to see cities like Liverpool and Manchester flourish! The anarchy that is ruling London, son, will cause us even more problems if it doesn't stop. I'll tell you what is going to happen. If I see a journalist within half a mile of this Police Station, I will personally make sure he's arrested and put away for obstructing the course of justice. And you solve this case within two weeks from now. I've had it. Completely.'

The Superintendent didn't say goodbye -he just shambled away. Ben stared at the door for a while and then shrugged. Two weeks wasn't that bad. If this had been a movie he would have been given twenty-four hours.

He took the first sheet from the pile and started to read. A girl had seen a very suspicious looking man in Leonard Street. He was...

And that's when the phone rang.

## 19.

'What do you mean, a hand grenade?' Ben Dixon could hardly speak. His throat had gone completely dry as soon as he understood what he was being told.

The line was silent for a moment, and all that he could hear was the mobile air conditioner. He cursed the bloody thing, because he hadn't heard the whole message thanks to the noise it was making.

Then the polite, slightly rigid voice came again.

'I want to believe that you don't understand me, because this is the first time I've called you direct. I will, therefore, repeat my message one more time: As from today I will have no mercy with anybody who is connected to a traffic violator. About two minutes ago I used a hand grenade to sentence the driver of a Volkswagen van and his fellow travelers for reckless driving. You will find their remains at the junction of Great Russell Street and Tottenham Court Road.'

'I didn't get your name.'

'I don't believe you. But even if you mean it, this will have to do. I don't like tracking devices. Good day.'

There was a short click, which was followed by the busy signal. Ben breathed heavily and blankly stared at the phone. A hand grenade?

He threw the handset back on the base, and the phone rang again immediately.

'Yes?'

The phone muttered.

'Yes, I just spoke to the halfwit myself. So what is it that you can tell me that will really make my day?'

The other party took about five minutes to explain a few things, by which time Ben had fully realized how big a bloodbath the cyclist had caused. There was a silence, and then the other party added something more to the information.

'What did you say?'

The last bit of information was repeated. Ben grunted.

'Do you have any idea how many bloody scooters there are in this godforsaken city? Do you have any idea what this means for the team? How much extra work this means? Why didn't you prepare me for this?'

He listened.

'Yes, I know what I said before. But…Oh, forget it. Thanks anyway.'

He threw the handset back and buried his head in his hands. A hand grenade on Tottenham Court Road; a cyclist who had decided to upgrade to a scooter. It had proven impossible to check each and every cyclist, and Ben couldn't even face considering trying something similar when it came to scooters. Ben cleared his throat and pictured Superintendent Steerer's face when he got the news. It didn't make him feel much better.

The phone rang again. Ben thought that news like this spread way too fast, and he braced himself for Steerer's next reprimand. He stretched his arm and picked up the phone reluctantly.

'Now what?'

Somebody spoke and Ben sat up straight. It wasn't Steerer. It was Robert Murdoch.

'Mister Murdoch, I know what's going on. The cyclist decided to tell me about this latest practical joke personally.'

Silence.

'So what did he tell you?'

Ben listened closely, but he heard nothing he didn't already know.

'Thank you, Mister Murdoch. I'll be in touch.'

He threw the handset back on the base and stared at the phone for a depressingly long time.

## 20.

"*Blackpool,*" Jim Jeremy wrote, "*is the worst thing that ever happened to England. Take the tower, for instance. That pathetic, completely misplaced Eiffel Tower lookalike that dominates the skyline (if you can think away the piers that is). Why hasn't there been a councilor yet who has proposed to flatten the whole place and start again, building something that the average seaside visitor will actually understand?*

*For let's be fair, you can't rate the intelligence of the average Blackpool visitor very highly, in fact, you can't really rate it too low. Come summer, winter, spring or autumn, they come in herds and like a drove they move along the piers and the promenade. If there are individuals who really want to enjoy the beach and the sea, they will have to plough their way through the crowds and fight the most repellant of people: children that make so much noise that jellyfish refuse to come close to the shore, even if the wind comes from the east. Fifteen stone women in tight leggings, parading like they are the next Miss England, where all they could ever be eligible for would be Miss Monster. Men with such huge bellies that the tide gets high as soon as they hit the water.*

*If you manage to survive that, you probably will suffocate from the Calvin Klein fumes that each and every Blackpool visitor considers to be the ultimate fragrance -using it so exuberantly that one immediately understands how it is possible that, even in times of crisis, sales figure for the stuff go up. Gulls drop dead because of it and it has become totally impossible to actually smell the sea.*

*Not to mention the fact that you can't actually see the sea anymore either. The crowd is too big, too massive, too bloody unmovable. Everyone happily presses his body against others and if you try to move away, the least you'll get is a foulmouthed remark, or a poke between the ribs.*

*It's a shame that the cyclist operates in London only. For if there is one place where people would be eligible for sentencing, it is Blackpool...*'


Robert rubbed his well-trimmed beard and gave Jim a piercing look.

'I'm not sure about this,' he said. 'I mean, the greater part is perfect, and I actually think that the greater part is completely true. But that bit about the cyclist could get us in trouble.'

'It's tapping into the same vein as 'Bicycle Race', Jim answered grumpily. 'It's as poignant as I can write them. What I'm trying to say is that people do get strange ideas. Our cyclist uses hand grenades, and only now people take him seriously. And it won't stop there, because there will be another idiot who thinks that there are too many people -period. Do you know what would happen if you threw a hand grenade into the crowd on the North Pier? It would be a stampede with tens of deaths as a result. We have to be aware, instead of ignorant.'

Robert re-read the column and used Jim's explanation to understand it. He felt ashamed that he had missed the point, that Jim's sarcasm was beyond him, at least this time it was. The man had grown into his new job and his self-confidence was now bigger than his ego. And then this column...it was like Jim was thinking along with the cyclist, as if he were connected to him in a way...Robert focused on the words and avoided looking at Jim, afraid that his thoughts would betray him.

The other side was that Jim was right. The hand grenade had abruptly ended the anarchy that had made London almost unlivable, but not all boldness had vanished. Indeed, people needed to realize that the danger was still very much looming.

'I think I get it,' Robert now said. He looked Jim straight in the eye now. 'I will have to edit a few bits, but your message is clear and well presented. It's just a matter of slightly changing the tone. That is, if you agree.'

'Of course,' Jim said. 'I'm the writer, you are the editor. Is there anything else?'

There wasn't, and he left the office quickly, leaving Robert alone with his thoughts. The column didn't really sit well with the editor, but the nagging feeling wasn't prominent enough to really make him worry.

## 21.

Ben Dixon hated stairs. He was born in an attic room on Stansfield Road and had grown up in a third floor flat on Stockwell Road. The building didn't even have a service elevator, and it had left him with a lifelong antipathy for walking the stairs. Going down was bad because the steps were too small, but going up was even worse because he had to drag his full weight with him as well -and he had always been a big boy. Ben didn't like to walk at all, to be fair. The tricycle beat walking, the bicycle beat the tricycle, the scooter beat the bicycle, he got his provisional driving license when he was seventeen, and he had hardly done anything without a car from his eighteenth birthday onward. His deepest wish was that one day Tesco would build a drive-through store in the London area, so he wouldn't even have to leave his car anymore to get his shopping done.

But, at this very moment, Ben had no choice. His calves had started hurting after he got up the second staircase, and this was only the beginning. As soon as he turned onto St. George's Road his courage had begun to leave him. He had forgotten that this whole bloody area was full of flats and porches with staircases leading up to front doors, instead of the other way around -which would have been much more police officer friendly.

Ben had considered ditching the whole neighbourhood search as a result of it, but he had realized that this wouldn't make a good impression on the young man he had appointed as his personal assistant -and who took his job really seriously.

This was the boy who had come up with the idea of a neighbourhood search in the first place. He had entered Ben's office one morning.

'Good morning, Sir. May I ask you something?'

'Only if you keep it short.'

'I was hoping you could give me some tips about how to conduct a neighbourhood search.'

'What kind of crime deserves it to have you doing a neighbourhood search?'

'There is a smooth talker operating around Elephant & Castle. He's selling morning after pills for men, at twenty pounds a piece. They turn out to be plain Paracetamol tablets, but a lot of people have been aggrieved by it nevertheless.'

'You're a new recruit, aren't you?'

'I am, sir. And, well, as I said, I think I could learn a lot from you and your experience.'

One thing Ben's experience had taught him, was to steer clear of neighbourhood searches wherever possible. All you would get were the latest rumours, but chances that you would get useful information were more than just remote.

But equally, Ben knew that his own investigation needed a breakthrough, because he experienced a paralysing lack of leads, despite the fact that he now had over forty detectives working for him. And since one of the cyclist's earlier acts of sentencing had taken place just off Elephant & Castle, it made sense to combine the two. So when this boy -he'd really have to ask him for his name one of these days- came to him with his request for help, Ben had a hunch and jumped in.

'I'll help you with your search,' he said. 'If you help me with mine. As it is, I still have some unfinished business around Elephant & Castle.'

The boy had glowed with pride and by now Ben was happy with his decision; the boy did three doors in the time Ben needed to do one.

Ben looked up along a new set of stairs, into the shadowy porch. The colour of the front door told him exactly what he would encounter next: an old hag who knew everything about everybody but who, 'I'm really sorry, sir', hadn't seen anything suspicious for the last seventy-five years. He sighed and started up the stairs. Ben Dixon hated old hags.

## 22.

'The Pothole"'s editorial staff was happy. The tabloid had managed to win a great segment of the market at the expense of it's competitors, and that had made them proud. 'The Pothole' was still the only paper that carried all the news about the cyclist first, because the man still called Robert Murdoch as soon as he struck again. The journalists were convinced that the way they dealt with the issues had been the main reason why the Londoners had jumped back into line, and that they were responsible for the new sense of safety that hung over the city.

Boldness had traded places with carefulness. The hand grenade hadn't missed its target, literally or figuratively speaking. Londoners finally understood that the cyclist, which was the way everybody still referred to him, was serious. At last they understood that the victims were chosen totally at random. The cyclist didn't care for race, sex, skin colour or religion. So far he had not touched any children, but everybody knew that it would only be a matter of time before he would extend his crusade to, at least, adolescents.

'Do as you're told,' returned to many households as a standard phrase in upbringing. 'Or the cyclist will get you next.'

The cyclist had become a basic ingredient in daily London life. And, although deeply rooted in fear, he had achieved what he had been aiming for: disciplined road users, and safe use of bicycle lanes and sidewalks.

*"The cyclist,"* Jim Jeremy, therefore, wrote, *"is quiet. It looks like he's vanished from the face of the earth. No longer do we find people with a small hole in their head because they were cycling on the pavement. No longer do we see anyone not using their lights after dusk. No longer do we see fog lights blinding us on the clearest of nights. I seems that we all have accepted that even the smallest of traffic violations can lead to an immediate death penalty.*

*You can't justify murder, period. Yet it is time that we begin to realize how deep we had been sinking. Just check the statistics -we now have the lowest number of road traffic victims since we started to record them. Irritation on the road has all but disappeared. We are scared, of course we are, afraid that we will be killed if we make so much of a mistake, yet at the same time we can look each other right in the eyes because we hardly make any mistakes anymore. That is a paradox -and an educational one.*

*I, too, can't wait to be able to cross the street without expecting a bullet. But the fear doesn't have to subside completely. When I was young, seeing a bobby was enough to make me behave. Officer's still had authority, and if you misbehaved, they'd punish you. These days we are on a first name basis with them. Is that really the way it should be like? Or are they still meant to keep order? If they want to regain their authority, now is the time to act. I know people won't like me for saying this, but the cyclist did bring back a sense of social standards and values we had long forgotten about...'*

Robert Murdoch tried to hide his unease. He wondered if he could actually get away with publishing this. It wasn't that he didn't agree with it, but he did think that it would lose the tabloid thousands of readers, and he feared that it could damage the very good relationship he had built with the Metropolitan Police.

Nobody wanted to live in fear. It didn't matter that traffic was safer than ever before. There was a looney on the loose with a gun, which he used at random.

But then again, pieces like this one would once again feed discussion groups and talk shows. 'The Pothole' was being mentioned time and time again for being the only tabloid that didn't shy away from publishing unpopular views as well as the more accepted ones, and the print runs did benefit from that.

Robert looked Jim in his greyish-blue eyes, that now had an almost obsessed twinkle in them. Was the man just trying to see how far he could go?

'Jim, listen. This may be all true, but you can't take sides with a murderer who has killed almost a hundred people, chases away tourists and is still very much on the run. That is asking for trouble.'

Jim bit his lip.

'I'm not sure about that,' he said. 'Just look at it from a realistic point of view. The city has never been safer. Better yet, people in other cities are beginning to behave better because they fear that he may have moved. I think everybody should realize that he alone managed to achieve what thousands of politicians and police officers couldn't.'

'I know that. But you can't call this a column! Two pieces like this one and you'll have lost all the credit you've built up over the past months.' He noticed the pale face that this remark caused, but before he could soften his message, Jim spoke.

'Can't you use it as an editorial then?' he queried. 'I'll write something about Christmas instead. That hasn't really hit the streets yet anyway. Even the adverts are slow. It's still the cyclist who makes the news.'

'You do that,' Robert said. He didn't want to waste too many words on this. 'You write something about Christmas. Indeed, at least you'll be the first one to do so.'

Jim muttered something, but he didn't speak up and he left the office quickly. Robert sighed with relief. Thankfully this had just blown over. He could see the justification in Jim strongly supporting the cyclist but he, Robert Murdoch, as an editor, had to think in the interest of 'The Pothole' as a whole.

Jim should stick to his cynicism -he was still the best in his field. But he had lost the plot when it came to the cyclist.

Robert rubbed his well-trimmed beard and read Jim's article again. He shook his head, took his red pen and started to edit the piece.

But then he stopped. He thought deeply for another minute and a faint smile appeared on his face. Maybe, they should just go for it after all...

## 23.

Ben Dixon hated it when he got stuck in investigation. What made him even angrier was that he knew, deep down inside, that somewhere in that huge pile of paper, in all those big files and scattered around notepads, the answer lay waiting.

He looked around his office. The 'London Jazz Festival' poster he had put up on the wall had been visible for exactly two weeks before he had to hide it behind more files. The walls were now completely hidden behind files, requests, accounts from eye witnesses, loose notes, newspapers, tabloids, weeklies and anything that could be remotely connected to the cyclist.

He focused on all those letters and figures and tried hard to think where, in that mix of dead people and witness statements, that one clue could be. There had to be a lead that could really take him forward, one trail, no matter how frail, that wouldn't lead to yet another grey shrew in another grey flat. He thought about the fruitless neighbourhood searches. While doing his bit around Elephant & Castle he did have quite a few good laughs because of the smooth operator and his morning after pills for men. The naivety of the mob had made his hopeless investigation look a little less desperate and he had felt relieved, seeing that his life wasn't as miserable as that of most of his fellow citizens. But hardly anybody had seen anything, or they had been so shocked when they saw the cyclist act, that they had buried what they had witnessed so deep in their brains they couldn't drag it out again.

But even the more likely witnesses weren't of any help in the hunt for the killer on two wheels. At least thirty people had witnessed the assault on the van in Tottenham Court Road, yet no two descriptions of the cyclist matched. The man had been described as a Belgian, a black man, Chinese, a white guy, a Russian, a Spaniard, an Italian, a German and a Hungarian. On top of that one witness had described him as a Pakistani with Jewish features. The colour of his coat ranged from plain white to purple with orange flowers ('I was thinking I wouldn't even have something like that as a table cloth'), one witness was 'absolutely certain' that the scooter had featured a sidecar. Everybody agreed that the man had been wearing glasses, but, again, that was as far as the similarities went. It had been sunglasses, but 'no, wait, it was the kind of glasses that reflect your own image' (so it had been sunglasses after all); the glasses had been round or octagonal, one lady was convinced the man had been wearing diving goggles. About half of the witnesses had mentioned a beard, but as could be expected, that ranged from a soul patch to a full untrimmed beard and moustache. Ben was still waiting for the picture from the sketch artist, but he was sure he would end up with a picture of somebody who'd look like a cross between Bruce Forsyth, Hannibal the Cannibal and Mickey Mouse.

The cyclist could, therefore, be quite sure that he wouldn't be recognized, so the chances that he would be caught because a witness would recognize him, were slim. Stella Johnson and Harry Powell, with two l's, had stuck to their statements, which had as many similarities as they had differences. They had also reconfirmed the name they said the man had used but, to be fair, after the fourth killing nobody had really bothered to listen to what that idiot with the gun was saying. People just tried to get away from the scene, and it usually took a lot of effort to convince them that they really needed to give a statement.

And those statements would surely be a blocked writer's dream: they were an interesting and fascinating collection of facts and fantasies, that cast a whole new light on the way the average Londoner lived his life.

There were too many suspects -or just not enough. It was clear that the cyclist was a man, but that only ruled out half the population. Ben had hoped that Mister Powell would betray himself, but the man actually was a parochial nervous asshole. He had coffee with the neighbours, bought his groceries at Tesco Metro, fumbled with his rings continuously and hardly ever left the house. His neighbours all had declared that this was the way the man, and his wife, had lived for years, and most of them had expressed doubts if Powell had any emotions at all. In short, Powell's behaviour during the interview had been completely normal -for him.

Still, the cyclist's name haunted Ben. He had heard it only once, when the cyclist had announced his hand grenade assault to him, but that stupid mobile air conditioner had prevented him from really understanding it. His hatred for electrical equipment had reached new heights because of it, but that didn't really help him. It was eating him, because he was more and more convinced that the name could, after all, harbour the very clue he was looking for.

His door opened and Superintendent Steerer entered the room. Ben was almost glad to see him. It seemed like months ago (which it was) since the man had given him two weeks to solve the case, but as the roads became safer his superior had cut him some slack, leaving him to stubbornly continue his investigation. But somehow, Ben figured that, by now, he would be running out of time. Steerer's face didn't promise any sweet talk.

'I can see that you are thinking,' Steerer said. He had given up on saying 'hello'. 'And I assume that I am about to hear your justification for the fact that you are sitting on your fat behind instead of being out there, arresting a murderer. I'm waiting.'

Ben got up and started to pace to and fro.

'I have no justification,' he admitted frankly. 'I know that we are overlooking something bleeding obvious, but I can't figure out what it is. It must be something small, a detail that has popped up only once and was never mentioned again.'

Steerer looked at him, frowning.

'Look, son, we can't hang around forever, waiting for you to get a hunch that will pay off. I've just gotten off the phone with Ed Balls, our respected Secretary of State for Children, Schools and Families. He wants to know when he can tell his target group that it is safe to go out and do the Christmas shopping. And, between you and me, he is becoming slightly impatient.'

Something clicked inside Ben's head. He slowly turned around to face Steerer and opened his mouth to say something, but his superior raised his hands in defence.

'No remarks, please. The Secretary is just as keen as everybody else to see this case solved before the festivities will start. But you can't blame Mister Balls for trying to push us a bit. After all, his electorate are the ones who make Christmas viable...what the devil is wrong with you now?'

'That name,' Ben muttered. 'That name...'

He felt like somebody had slapped him in the face when he made the connection. Galls? Balls? Could that really be true?

Ben turned around and started digging into the piles of paper without any kind of strategy. He had forgotten all about Superintendent Steerer, because somewhere in this huge pile of nonsense was a piece of information that may not have been nonsense all along.

Ben Dixon hated it when he couldn't find what he was looking for.

## 24.

I didn't expect that I would be so empty once my mission was completed. I just can't get used to it. It is such a relief to be able to cycle everywhere and only have to be alert at junctions and crossings. But my life has become so empty. When the Londoners were at their ignorant best, I was serving a noble purpose. I taught them the rules, the laws. I reinstated their respect for order and authority. That was rewarding in itself. I thought.

But where is my reward? Why are they still out there, looking for me? I haven't had to punish anybody for quite some time now! They should be grateful for the order that is now in place on the public roads. But the opposite is true! They have issued a reward for anyone who can arrest me, or gives the police the golden clue! So much for gratefulness. Nobody mentions that I made their job so much easier for them. And the press aren't any better. Why do they still picture me as a madmen who deserves to be thrown off the London Eye without a parachute? How can people be so cruel? If you really need to kill somebody, you have to make it as quick and painless as possible. You must aim right, and you mustn't hesitate. Like this. Two shots, two holes, three millimeters apart. This is alright. I'll leave the dummy like this. Those two holes give her something extra.

There is so much injustice in the world. People are so dense. Traffic is conveniently controlled these days, but what about the rest of our society? Innocent people are being harassed after dark. Or worse. Look at this item. It's used as filler on page nine, but still... "Police are hunting four men who carried out a sickening attack in Enfield last night. Their victim, who had just gone out for a walk because he couldn't sleep, was left with multiple fractures after they launched their attack on him at a bus stop on Slades Hill."

And what does the public do? Nothing! And the government? Even less! They tell us that it can't go on like this, that things really have to change. They all express their disgust in the six o'clock news, and then go home, open up an expensive bottle of wine and tell the wife that people are overreacting and that it's not as bad as everybody says it is. And the country becomes more unsafe with every sip they take.

It's a good thing I am going to check out my new apartment tomorrow. It's different from what I'm used to, but it will do. Three rooms, close to the city center, central heating. And I like the new neighbourhood. Lots of foreigners, artists and students, and a terrific market within cycling distance. Seafood, foreign fruits, fresh vegetables...it'll definitely do.

Should I grow a beard, or is a clean-shaven face better? Do I have to worry about that? Maybe not yet, but it is good to think about it every now and then. I don't want to have to face any surprises now, not when I've come this far. One must know when to make the right decisions. I can still stay put and pull the wool over everybody's eyes. But if I prepare my retreat at the same time, I can leave whenever I please, and start a new life wherever I please. And starting anew is a lot easier than staying put and not getting caught in the end. I've done well. I've got everything under control.

25.

Robert Murdoch was removing his condom when the doorbell rang.

'Will you get it?' he said to Debbie. 'Just tell him I'm coming.'

'I thought you came already,' she replied and she walked out of the bedroom.

'Hey!' Robert shouted. 'Wait!'

Debbie reappeared and Robert threw her one of his buttoned shirts. 'Put this on. Let's make at least a bit of a decent impression on the guy.'

Debbie shrugged, but put on the shirt. No man had ever complained when she answered the door naked, but this was Robert's place, so she played by his rules. Besides, the shirt made her look terrifically sexy.

Ben Dixon enjoyed having a moment to look at one of the cafés where a lovely waitress was cleaning the tables, but he was also somewhat annoyed. He hated it when people made him wait, especially when they knew that he was coming. Furthermore, he was a bit jealous. He knew how expensive these Berkely Square apartments were, he knew there was no way he could ever afford something like that, and yet, this journalist was the proud owner of one of them. Ben had never realized that doing a bit of sensationalist writing could be so lucrative, and he wondered if it was too late for a career change. His eyes moved a few yards on, where a man was trying to pull open a door, which was obviously jammed. The noise he made bounced back from the building's facades and provoked displeased comments from passers-by; but the man had clearly no intention of letting go before that door had given way, or was torn to pieces.

Ben's gaze went from the waitress to the man and he had almost forgotten that he was waiting when behind him the lock was turned, and the door opened.

He turned around and gazed at the woman in the door opening for a full minute. She looked back as uninterested as she could be.

'Hello, dad,' Debbie finally said. 'To what do I deserve the honour? Or are you really here to talk to Robert?'

Ben looked at his daughter with his mouth half open. It wasn't so much her physical presence that struck him, but the fact that he never realized that Debbie had actually reached the age of consent, and hence could do what she damned well pleased. He looked at her for another couple of seconds and decided that he would disinherit her completely, first thing in the morning. You should never run into members of your family when you were at work. That could only lead to tragedy.

Debbie hadn't changed her pose.

'Do you want to come in? Or do you want me to call him out here? In that case I must warn you: he's not very good with cold.'

Ben pulled himself together and went inside. He went straight for the first door he saw.

'That's the bedroom, dad,' Debbie said innocently. The living room is a floor down.'

'Mister Dixon.' Robert proffered his hand and Ben rudely rejected it. 'Welcome to my humble home. My apologies for me being underdressed, but my time is scarce so I have to grab my opportunities when they present themselves.'

Ben looked at Debbie.

'That's an interesting way to describe it,' he grumbled 'Can we talk somewhere privately? This doesn't concern her.'

Debbie giggled.

'Don't worry. The only thing that concerns me is something that you are not likely to be interested in.'

Robert touched Ben's arm.

'Let us go to my study,' he said. 'And then please tell me what I can do for you.'

Ben Dixon hated unequal situations. Here he was, dressed in a suit and matching tie, facing a man who was wearing nothing but a, too tight, bathrobe, and in the next room there was his own daughter, dressed in an oversized shirt and nothing else, shamelessly watching some kind of adult channel. Ben decided to keep the conversation as short as possible, but some things had to be asked.

'Mister Murdoch, I do apologize for me intruding. I was willing to wait until you were back at your office, but my superior...'

Robert discarded the apology. He knew all about Superintendent Steerer's slightly bizarre character traits, and one of the freelance cartoonists had used him to create a brilliant caricature who had his own daily cartoon, and who was very popular with the readers. Ben knew that, too. He had seen too much of that tabloid lately.

'Mister Murdoch. During my investigation I have found that The Potho...your newspaper has published quite a few articles, all of them from the same angle. In the case of the cyclist, that leads me to asking you for a clarification.'

That went well, Ben thought. Until he looked at Robert Murdoch again. Despite Ben's effort, the editor was totally unimpressed.

'I haven't got a clue what you are talking about,' Robert said. 'Can you be a bit more specific? Do you have any idea how many articles land on my desk each day?'

'No,' Ben said. 'But I expected your reply. So I took the liberty of bringing some clippings. Like this one. "We've got Balls." A great pun, mister Murdoch. And possibly the cheapest of ways to ridicule a newly appointed Secretary of State.'

'I though you said that you didn't read our paper?' Robert asked. Ben gave him a cold stare.

'I have every intention to stop as soon as is possible, Mister Murdoch. But, if it's for a just cause, one sometimes has to temporarily set his principles aside. You, too, don't always play by the rules, or do you, when you know that a bit of cheating may benefit your print run?'

'I always play by the rules,' Robert said flatly. 'That's called professional ethics.'

'Whatever, Mister Murdoch. But this is your second article about the cyclist. "He's got Balls." Well chosen again, no doubt.'

'Reader's memories don't go back very far, Mister Dixon. Nor do journalists'. News is fast. It fades before it can grow old.'

'I wish I could believe you. But I don't believe in coincidences. The cyclist mentioned his name when he called me, Mister Murdoch. I was caught off-guard and didn't hear it well. During our investigations people came up with all sorts of names, all sounding similar, but none of them exclusive. But then this article, this screaming header. A pun, again, and, I believe, based on a name you knew. A name you knew indeed, even when you gave me that letter. And now this, Mister Murdoch. Your latest editorial. It's almost an open invitation to the authorities to show their 'balls' and give up the search for the cyclist. Do you really believe that no one would raise an eyebrow -or have a question or two?'

Robert wanted to say something, but Ben raised his hand.

'I'll tell you something, Mister Murdoch. You acted co-operatively, but you know more than you told me. And either you or your newspaper is protecting the cyclist. Well, Mister Murdoch, either you are going to tell me everything, or I'll take you into custody. And you know what happens when Superintendent Steerer gets his hands on a journalist these days.'

Robert rubbed his well-trimmed beard.

I think I'm going to shave, he thought. And then he began to talk.

## 26.

*"All things considered,"* Jim Jeremy wrote, *"Jesus was the first Santa Claus. It is therefore quite remarkable that the Church declines the commercial opportunities that come with it. This is a major opportunity for the Church to get right back into the heart of civilization. I admit that it sounds ambitious, but it's not as impossible as it seems. The Church could launch its own brand of communion wafers for daily use, and build special offers around each different season or, if they wish, holy event. In the build up to Christmas they could market them with different handcrafted icons which, once you've collected them all, depict the story of the Nativity in a beautiful way. Something similar could be done over Easter, depicting the Apostles while they're out rabbit hunting..."*

Robert nodded approvingly. He caught Jim's inquisitive look and said: 'Is there something wrong?'

Jim shook his head, but his frown remained.

'No. I just have this funny feeling something has changed. Never mind...

Robert looked at his column.

'This is great piece to round it all up, wouldn't you agree?'

'Round it up? Am I fired?'

'No,' Robert replied and he raised his hands in defence. 'But we want to give our readers some space in the last weeks of the year. Make them feel appreciated. Do you know how much unsolicited mail we receive?'

Jim bit his lip.

'I can imagine it's quite a bit,' he said. 'I mean, you wouldn't believe the crap that I find in my mail box every morning. Once people know that you are a writer...'

'I think that some stories are actually quite good,' Robert said. 'And we want to publish them. This is the time of the year that we loosen up a bit. Everybody is happy and sociable, and they like it if we do things like that.'

Jim snorted. Robert remembered him saying that he didn't like amateurs, period. If somebody had something to say he should either make it his profession, or pass it on to someone who had already made it his. And, beyond that, they shouldn't interfere with the press. The mob was too grey, too stupid and too narrow-minded to have an opinion.

'But about you,' Robert returned to the conversation. 'I think you've deserved a decent vacation. Your editing was perfect, your columns were outstanding. You have a good time over the next few weeks, and I'd like to see you back at work on the fourth of January. Here.' He opened a desk drawer and took out an envelope, which he handed to Jim. Jim opened it, saw two plane tickets and a hotel voucher, and looked up questioningly.

'A two-week trip to Mexico? What have I done to deserve that?'

'They are questioning my expenses claims,' Robert replied. 'And I don't want to end up like some of our MP's. So if I divide it equally among the staff, everything is according to the rules. And as I said: I think you deserve it.'

Jim bit his lip. Robert remained calm, but inwardly he cursed Jim's paranoia.

'What will happen here when I'm away? Did I forget some kind of anniversary? A birthday? Any other milestone?'

'No, honestly, you haven't forgotten anything, and nothing is going to happen. I truly believe that you deserve this trip. You have done a great job this year. And nothing will change. We will publish reader's stories, and I don't think I'd do you a big favour asking you to do the editing.'

'No,' Jim said. 'You are quite right there. Whatever you say, Robert. I'll fly to Mexico. I don't think I'll have much trouble having a good time without 'The Pothole'. Was that it?'

Robert breathed more freely and he smiled.

'Yes, that's all. Have fun. And I expect you fully re-charged and,' he pointed at the column on his desk, 'back, sharp as razor, in the New Year. Do you have somebody to join you?'

'I don't think so. The only decent company I can think of, will definitely not be able to come. It would make her husband too suspicious. I'll just check out all the different brands of tequila while I watch the bronzed beauties. Merry Christmas.'

He was gone before Robert had returned the greeting.

The chief-editor stared at the column on his desk for a long, long time, followed by another fifteen minutes in which he just stared at the phone. Eventually he picked up the phone, checked a business card that was lying on his desk, and called the mobile number that was on it. While he waited he confidently rubbed his clean-shaven chin.

'Mister Dixon? Robert Murdoch. The articles you gave me? It appears that your theory was right. They were all written by the same person...'

## 27.

Ben Dixon hated final conclusions. Not because of the conclusions themselves, for he was absolutely crazy about solved mysteries, but because of the feeling that always followed a solved crime; the huge emptiness that would swallow him as soon as he crashed on his couch, because all the stress, excitement and frustration was gone, and all that was left was tedious paperwork. He invariably disappeared for two days to go on a binge, only to return to his job on the morning of the third day- still completely hung over. The only good thing was that, by then, another case had usually landed on his desk, and the whole circus could begin again.

Now that he was close to wrapping the case up, Ben silently admitted that he had felt a bit of admiration for the cyclist, whose influence still hadn't faded yet. Most people were still very cautious and sensible in traffic because the cyclist still hadn't been arrested. Tomorrow's headlines would undoubtedly provoke another outburst of anarchy, but London would at least have a fear-free Christmas to look forward to. And, as far as Ben was concerned, they would hang the cyclist from St. Paul's dome without even so much of a pro-forma trial.

He closed the file he had been reading in. It wouldn't be long before the cyclist would no longer be anonymous, or hiding behind his fake name. He switched off the lights and left his office, but when he saw Superintendent Steerer in the hall it was too late to turn around.

'Could you come into my office for a moment, son?' his superior asked him, very friendly. 'I have something for you.'

Ben grumbled, but duly followed the superintendent into his room.

'Do sit down,' Steerer said, pointing at an old and battered desk chair. Ben lowered himself and watched Steerer sitting down in his more than comfortable leather seat. Ben thought of his own chair, covered with plastic, and concluded that the class system was still very much alive.

'I must apologize,' Steerer said and Ben had to hold on to his chair in order not to tumble over in amazement. 'I now understand why your investigation moved so slowly. I had no idea that you were dependent on the judge's ruling, and even if I had, I couldn't have sped it up. But there is good news, finally. This came in for you, only ten minutes ago.'

He handed Ben an official document and Ben read it. It was the court order he'd been waiting for, ruling that he was allowed to tap Robert Murdoch's phone without consent. Starting day...tomorrow, when all would be over.

He nevertheless folded the document carefully, and put it in his inside pocket.

'I wanted to surprise you,' he now said. 'But since we're here...we have found the trail we were looking for. We'll have the cyclist behind bars within twenty-four hours.'

Superintendent Steerer's face broke into a terrifying smile.

'Really? Even without...' he pointed at Ben and the detective nodded.

'We've worked overtime, sir, time and time again. Everybody has done their utmost, and I'm sure you won't be disappointed.'

Steerer nodded his head in excitement and Ben wished he had earplugs to shut out the blubbering sound of his triple chins.

'I knew you would do it,' Steerer said. 'It was the file, wasn't it? You've checked it again, right?'

Ben made a gesture that could mean anything.

'I'm proud of you,' Steerer continued. 'And as soon as everything is behind us, I'll buy you dinner. Do you like escargots?'

Ben was shocked, and he wondered what had happened to the original reward program. He shook his head and left the room. Ben Dixon hated dinners with his superiors.

## 28.

'Don't!' Ben hissed when the female constable was about to ring the doorbell. 'If he's not at the airport already, the guy will have some kind of escape plan. When he hears the doorbell at five in the morning, he'll be on the roof before we've climbed the stairs. Here. I have a universal master key. The only useful present I have ever been given -by a friend who used to work with MI5. Try it.'

They tried the key, and within ten seconds the lock sprung. The door opened without a squeak. Ben looked inside and smiled happily. He knew this type of building quite well. Three stories, rented out to different people, sharing one front door, and one back door only.

'You take the back door,' he whispered to the second constable he had brought with him, and the man hurried away.

'Third floor,' Ben whispered. 'You go first.'

The female constable started up the stairs. The boy -Ben reminded himself that he should really ask his name one of these days- went second, and Ben closed the ranks. One step creaked when Ben stood on it and he held his breath for a moment, but nothing moved and the house remained completely silent.

A door opened on the second floor. A man in a shiny, glittering blue jogging suit, carrying his running shoes in his hands, appeared. He was unshaven and looked like he had just woken up. He looked at the police officers and put a finger on his lips.

'Be quiet!' he hissed without showing any respect. 'People are still sleeping in there!'

Ben summoned him with his hands to get out of the way. The man looked around once more, but quietly continued his way downstairs, and went outside. The front door closed without a sound.

A small ray of light came from underneath the door on the third floor. Ben sighed. This was beginning to look good. He could hear a radio playing and he hummed along for a second. He knew this song.

He raised his arm and banged on the door. There was no response. The light was steady, and the radio kept playing. He drew his gun, and his colleagues followed his example.

This time they didn't need the master key. The door was unlocked, and they entered the apartment, guns raised, prepared to fire at anything or anybody.

They didn't have to, there was nobody home. Ben made his way to the bedroom. The bed was perfectly made and, like the rest of the apartment, looked like it hadn't been used for a while.

'Go through it,' Ben motioned. 'But don't make a mess. Grab everything that may be of interest. Pictures, diaries, letters...'

His attention was drawn to a drawer underneath the bed. He wrapped a handkerchief around his wrist and went for it, while his colleagues began searching the living room.

The drawer was empty and when Ben pulled it, it came out without a fight. Ben lost his balance and hit the floor hard. The drawer softly bumped into his behind and rolled back a few inches. The constable who came running to check the noise out, bit her lip in order not to burst out laughing.

Ben quickly got to his feet again.

'You keep looking for anything. I'm going to have a chat with the people next door about their friendly neighbour. They'll be awake by now anyway.'

He went down the stairs and knocked on the door of the second floor apartment. No answer came, but the sound of the radio was more prominent. Ben knocked again, and again, and finally tried the doorknob. The door was unlocked and the door swung open, as if it really wanted him to come in.

The first thing he saw was the window-dummy. On the floor beside it was an old typewriter -a Triumph, by the look of it. And from the portable cassette-player on the table came the song he had been humming along with only minutes ago. Now, of course, he could also hear the words he had heard Mick Jagger sing so often, and his stomach roared when he listened: "...I knew she was going to meet her connection/At her feet was her footloose man...You can't always get what you want/No you can't always get what you want..." Over and over again. Somebody had painstakingly put this tape together.

'If you try sometimes,' Ben grumbled, 'You will get what you want, because it's what you bloody need. You just wait, Jeremy. Constable!'

'Yes, sir?'

'Get on the scrambler and tell them that the suspect is still on the loose. He's dressed in a blue tracksuit. We'll need more men to comb the area.'

'The man on the stairs, sir?'

'I'm afraid so, constable.'

Ben went back into the apartment. Like the one on the third floor it used to be divided into two rooms, but this one had been reshaped into a studio.

Ben examined the two holes in the dummy, and noticed the traces of the repairs that had been done as well -the plaster, the new coat of varnish. He whistled. Murdoch had been right. Jim Jeremy was the cyclist, without a doubt. He had been right in their face all along, and nobody had ever guessed. Looking at the dummy, Ben thought that Jeremy could always try a career as a repairman. They would probably have more than enough for him to do in Wormwood Scrubs -or whatever hellhole they would eventually put him into.

'Uhm, Chief Inspector?'

Ben didn't like the sound of that at all. He rushed to the corridor. The constable was there, holding a blue tracksuit and a fake beard in his hands.

'What is it?'

'I found this in the street. Where...uhm...the car was...'

Ben froze for a moment, and then sprinted to the window. It was true, though. Chatham Street was quiet and empty. And there was no sign of the Metropolitan BMW.

He rested his head against the window sill, growled long and deep, and began counting from one to one hundred-thousand.

Ben Dixon hated to be outsmarted.

*"Jim Jeremy,"* Jim Jeremy wrote, *"was a decent name for a decent character. But a name is only a name is only a name...and looks may be deceiving. I'm sure you will come up with a police sketch that will nicely capture my characteristics as they were when you knew me. But I may have worn coloured lenses. I may have used cotton cushions to change the appearance of my cheeks. And were the cyclist's looks real?*

*Is his hair really black? Naturally curly, maybe? Does he have any hair at all?*

*I knew you were on my tail, for whatever the public may say, I am a good journalist. I knew when to listen to my gut, and I'm happy to see that I was right -as I have been right all along.*

*Franklin Theodore Balls was another decent name, and not just because it was such an obvious fake that everybody took it for real. I thank you all for only being able to make the right connections after I had decided it was time to call it a day. My deepest gratitude goes out to Robert, who was so keen on pleasing the Metropolitan Police that he did me the biggest favour of them all -by blanking the name out of the only document that could have given me away.*

*I don't feel the urge to defend myself or say anything truly incriminating. But I do ask you this, once more: will you be able to counter the loss of decent social standards and values as effectively as the cyclist has done?*

*I will never forget you, nor will I forget the apologetic expression on your face when I told you to be quiet. It was worth taking the risk. But then again, I didn't really feel like going to the airport anyway...*

*My time is scarce and I'll end this letter now. I wish you a very pleasant life. Sweet dreams, and don't worry. The cyclist will watch over you.*

*With the kindest regards,*

*F.T. Balls aka Jim Jeremy aka ???????*

The letter had been delivered at the Agar Street Police Station by a ten year old boy at around eight o'clock in the morning. Naturally, it didn't bear a signature.

Superintendent Steerer watched Ben from his comfortable leather chair and pushed a box of cigars towards him.

'Have a cigar, son,' he said jovially. 'You almost had him, didn't you?'

Ben hated cigars, but he knew when not to refuse them. He lit one and thought that at least he wouldn't have to spent the evening having escargots with his superior. There was justice after all.

'Yes,' he said. 'But it doesn't get us anywhere. I still blame myself for just letting him go his way.'

'You have nobody to blame,' Steerer tried to cheer him up. 'I've seen the file and the facts. Nothing indicated that these two floors were rented by one and the same individual.'

'That is true, but I am a police officer. I have to expect the unexpected, especially when I'm entering the house of a suspected murderer...'

'Son, don't make it too hard on yourself,' Steerer interrupted him. 'I became Superintendent without ever making one arrest! There is hope for you, believe me. Do you have anything planned for Christmas yet?'

Ben froze in his chair and forcefully pushed back an urge to retch. He stuttered an ultimately vague story about family ties, festive days and more of that nonsense, hoping that he sounded convincingly enough. He did, for Steerer didn't actually listen to his reply. Instead he gave him a story of the importance of Christmas, especially under the current circumstances. He used so many clichés that Ben couldn't help but thinking that the man had broken a world record right there.

When he finally left Steerer's room and went down the stairs, he felt guilt creeping up inside him. He checked his watch, took a deep breath and already he had forgotten the thoughts he had a few days ago, when he was waiting for Robert Murdoch to open his door. Ben stepped into the cold winter evening. He crossed the street, and had to jump aside because he almost got hit by a speeding scooter - the passenger of which giving him the finger when he shouted at them; then, reluctantly started walking towards Covent Garden.

For the moment, everything was back to normal, and there was still time to buy Debbie a Christmas present.

# Epilogue

Arndale Market was busy. People shuffled from stall to stall. There was no moving space, and by the looks of it, hardly any breathing space either.

The old man tried to find a lettuce that was small enough for one.

'What will it be, grandpa?' the seller said. 'Is that all? The cauliflower is really good.'

'Thank you, but no,' the old man said. 'I don't eat cauliflower. It's bad for your ears. I'd like a pound of carrots though, a pound of potatoes and three onions.'

The old man watched the merchant picking the vegetables, when he felt a sudden push. He sensed the hand that slid in his back pocket and he turned around with remarkable ease, given his age. Before him stood a young man with a very unfriendly face and piercing eyes.

'You want something?' he barked at the old man.

'My wallet, please,' said the man, softly but very clearly.

The boy cast him a haughty look, but the expression on his face changed when the old man slowly brought his hand towards his inside pocket. The boy didn't think twice. He dropped the wallet, turned around and wrestled his way out of the crowd. The old man smiled, picked up his wallet and took the plastic bag out of his inside pocket.

'Would you please put it in here?' he asked the merchant, who hadn't noticed anything at all.

'Sure, grandpa,' the man answered and he winked at the smiling bystanders. 'We have to care about the environment, don't we?'

A few yards away stood a tall, lean and bald man. He had watched the scene and now shook his head over the injustice done. If it had been him, he couldn't help thinking, things definitely would have gone a bit differently.

His hand touched his chest, and he took comfort from the 3032 Tomcat that was waiting patiently inside his pocket.

The man smiled.

His time would most certainly come…

…again.

Frank Alexander – The Cyclist